Kevin Malone ... ... and asked, "Are you with us, Longarm?"

Before Longarm could answer a bullet crashed through the casement he'd been closing. The crown and broad brim of his Stetson caught a heap of the shattered glass as the hot lead almost parted his hair. Then he'd shoved the startled Phaedra Thorne off the far end of the bench they'd been sharing and thrown himself atop her as another shot showered them with more busted glass.

Kevin Malone made the deputies shooting back hold their fire before their wild fusillade could do too much damage to downtown Durango. In the ringing silence that ensued Longarm rolled off the English girl, his own .44-40 in hand. He told her he was sorry if he'd scared her. She dimpled up at him to reply it had been the sod outside who'd had her worried.

Malone asked Longarm who the sniper could have been out to get.

Longarm dryly replied, "I'll ask him when we catch him!"

TABOR EVANS

LONGARM

AND THE DURANGO DOUBLE-CROSS

JOVE BOOKS, NEW YORK

LONGARM AND THE DURANGO DOUBLE-CROSS

A Jove Book / published by arrangement with
the author

PRINTING HISTORY
Jove edition / March 1998

The Penguin Putnam Inc. World Wide Web site address is
http://www.penguinputnam.com

ISBN: 0-515-12244-0

A JOVE BOOK®
Jove Books are published by The Berkley Publishing Group, a member
of Penguin Putnam Inc.,
200 Madison Avenue, New York, New York 10016.
JOVE and the "J" design are trademarks
belonging to Jove Publications, Inc.

PRINTED IN THE UNITED STATES OF AMERICA

10 9 8 7 6 5 4 3 2 1

LONGARM

AND THE
DURANGO DOUBLE-CROSS

Chapter 1

The stage route twisting through the dry canyon country west of Durango was one of the longer ones left as horsepower gave way to the Iron Horse and Singing Wire. As her sun-crackled Concord coach grated to an unexpected stop in the middle of nowhere, Miss Phaedra Thorne of the *Illustrated London News* looked up from her sketch pad to be met by the puzzled stares of her fellow passengers, a portly Mormon elder and his two younger wives.

The Latter-Day Saint replied to Phaedra's unspoken question with, "I don't know. We're at least seven miles short of our last change of teams at the La Plata Station."

Mormon elders were not supposed to comment on the forbidden charms of petite, Gentile brunettes wearing shantung travel dusters, expensive summer hats of straw dyed to match their wearer's hazel eyes, or horn-rimmed glasses that only made such eyes seem bigger and deeper.

Their shotgun messenger opened the right-hand door to say, "Ever'body out. We're packing a heavy strongbox and heaps of mail today, and our Jehu doubts our mules could make the grade ahead unless we lighten the load a mite."

The Mormon elder tried, "See here, the four of us have paid good money to *ride*, not *walk*, to the railhead in Durango!"

To which the shotgun messenger replied in an easygoing but final way, "It ain't but two or three furlongs to the top of the rise, and we won't make you get out and walk again, this side of Durango."

The four of them got out, with the shotgun messenger lending the ladies a grimy helping hand, as if passengers had any choice about such matters. Phaedra was glad she'd left her sketch pad and pencil on the seat when her two carpetbags thumped to the dusty trail near her high-button shoes and she glanced up to see their driver ready to drop the big Saratoga trunk of her fellow passengers.

As the portly Mormon and both his young wives protested with some vigor, the shotgun messenger beside them soothed, "Don't holler afore you're hurt, old son. I'll grab one end as Lem slides her over the rail. Then you can grab the other, see?"

The older man braced himself to catch the weight, even as he let fly with, "You surely don't expect these ladies and myself to carry all this baggage over a quarter mile, uphill, do you?"

As the two of them lowered the heavy trunk to the dry grit just off the trail, the shotgun messenger said, "I have to leg it too. I just now said we had to lighten the load."

Phaedra Thorne bent gracefully to pick up her two lighter bags, murmuring, "Next time I'll go the long way round, by railway!"

As if he'd heard her laconic cliché, the Jehu seated grandly up above them cracked his whip and the now much lighter Concord lurched forward to take a good run at the rising trail ahead.

The Mormon and the shotgun messenger picked up the trunk between them, and all five trudged onward and upward through the settling dust of two dozen hooves and four steel-rimmed wheels. Phaedra was glad she was wearing her raw silk duster over her summer calico frock as she tasted the ashes of a long-dead sea on her dry tongue. When she walked more to windward with her bags the alkali gave way to what could be taken for the musty medicinal odors of an apothecary shop in need of a good airing. She'd understood for some time now why the Yanks called those silvery-gray growths sagebrush, or why they called that knee-high spinach creosote bush. There was something else out there that smelled very much like licorice root and she'd never liked that smell either.

The myopic young newspaper illustrator glanced up and around when she heard a distant pistol shot. Their coach had come to a stop in a notch between chaparral covered rimrocks up ahead. The shotgun messenger helping the portly Mormon elder to Phaedra's left said, "Reckon Lem is anxious to drive on, now that he's made the grade. So leave us pick 'em up and lay 'em down and we'll soon have you off this dusty trail and complaining about the service aboard the D&RGW Railroad."

They struggled on. But they hadn't made it halfway up the rise when the shotgun messenger stopped them to call ahead, "Are you all right, Lem?"

They could all see their Jehu, facing the other way in his high seat as he neither replied nor even turned his head toward them.

The shotgun messenger lowered his end of the Mormon's trunk as he muttered, "You all stay here whilst I have a closer look."

The older man lowered his own end, quietly mentioning, "I have a Sharp's .52 in this trunk and I know how to use it."

The shotgun messenger said, "Get it out and get these ladies to some cover, then. I'll find out how come Lem's acting so peculiar."

Then he drew his six-gun and moved on up the slope,

3

circling out through the stirrup-high chaparral as he called once more to the oddly frozen driver seated in plain sight.

The Mormon elder said something softly to his young wives, then called out to the more distant visitor from London, "You'd best get over to that same clump of catclaw, miss."

So Phaedra was crossing the trail with her bags when they heard another distant shot. When she looked that way their shotgun messenger was nowhere to be seen. But a whispy white cloud of smoke was drifting above the chaparral close to where she'd last spied him.

As she joined the two Mormon girls behind the aptly named catclaw brush, she saw that their husband had opened their trunk to haul out a huge buffalo rifle. One of his wives called out for him to stay out of any Gentile fights he hadn't been invited to. But he rose with surprising grace for such a fat old man and moved up the trail with the muzzle of his single-shot rifle leading the way at waist level.

Phaedra asked his nearest Mormon wife what on earth was going on. The ashen-faced American girl replied, "Indians or road agents. We get both out here in the canyon lands. From the way the menfolk are acting, I'd wager road agents."

"Road agents?" the English girl asked.

The local resident replied, "Outlaws. I reckon you'd call them highwaymen where you come from." Then she called out, "Hiram, come back here and let them settle it amongst themselves!"

Then all three women flinched as a fusillade of shots rang out. The portly Mormon elder spun in place like a top winding down, with his two wives screaming. As he fell, the weirdest sight the well-traveled Phaedra Thorne of the *Illustrated London News* had ever seen strode out of the gun smoke and chaparral just up the trail to finish the downed man off with one of the smoking six-guns he was waving.

4

On second glance the pistol-packing killer seemed some sort of Red Indian to the English girl. He was stark naked, save for the gun belt around his waist and the keg-shaped, garishly painted, feather collared mask that hid his entire head. His tawny skin was painted or perhaps tattooed in a sort of paisley-print pattern of dotted lines.

As he stepped out on the trail they saw a turtle shell rattle was lashed to his right calf. There were sleigh bells around his decorated or disfigured left thigh. His full erection was painted or tattooed to resemble a snake. The nearest Mormon girl keeled over in a dead faint as she spied that staring at her over the body of her dead husband.

Phaedra Thorne dropped and started crawling, fast. She didn't know whether the killer had seen her or not through the eye slits of his grotesque mask. It was very clear she'd just been face-to-face with Death Incarnate!

The frightened visitor from London was almost a furlong off in the chaparral when she missed her glasses and sobbed, "Bloody stars and garters! I'll never get over the stile tonight without me specs!"

She began to retrace her crawl through the pungent brush. A button cactus pricked one groping hand before she felt her way back to her glasses, wiped them clean enough on her now aptly named duster, and put them back on to discover with a start that her hat dangled from a branch of catclaw just beyond.

She sat on her knees in the chaparral, pinning her hat back atop her dark upswept hair as, somewhere nearby, a bird began an unfamiliar but carefree sounding song. Phaedra craned higher, to see nobody at all between her and the distant figure of their Jehu. He'd climbed down from the driver's seat of their stagecoach to move down the slope toward her.

Phaedra rose, cautiously, to move back to the trail. As she did so she saw the two Mormon girls had broken cover to head the same way. Then they were racing for their dead

5

husband, sprawled on the trail with his rifle. Phaedra saw the Jehu had paused by something else in the chaparral across the way and cut that way to join him.

But as she came closer the driver called, "You'd best stay yonder, ma'am. They got old Tom, here. That murderous kachina dancer shot him in the back, with his shotgun atop the rise in its boot!"

The visitor from London replied, "How awful! You say that creature just now was a . . . kazoo dancer?"

"Kachina, ma'am," the Jehu corrected, adding, "gussied up like a pagan Pueblo Indian god or goddess. The other two who popped out of the brush at the top of the rise were dressed more Mex, with feed sacks over their heads. Lord knows where they're headed just now with our strongbox. What are them other ladies fussing about, down the slope a piece, ma'am?"

She told him. He spat and said, "I'd be obliged if you'd comfort 'em whilst I get all the baggage back on board, ma'am. I'll run us on to La Plata Station. They'll send a buckboard back here for both these old boys."

She asked, "You mean, just leave both bodies out here unguarded and uncared for?"

The Jehu quietly replied, "I cared for Tom Cartier. He was my pal as well as my shotgun messenger. Nobody can hurt a dead man, and none of you ladies would thank me, come supper time, for making you ride with two shot-up cadavers that far in this weather."

Phaedra gulped and decided not to argue the point. The Jehu seemed to be trying to be gentle with the two sobbing sudden widows as they all climbed back into the coach at the top of the rise a few minutes or a million years later.

Phaedra Thorne had managed herself and her carpetbags without any help. It was only after they were under way again that she noticed her sketch pad and pencil on the floor between the facing seats.

She picked it up and tore away the landscape she'd been

working on to start all over while the coach swayed and jolted behind the trotting mules. One of the Mormon girls across from her was sobbing on the shoulder of her tight-lipped and dry-eyed companion in misery. That one stared for a time with distaste at Phaedra's rapid pencil before she bitterly asked whether Phaedra was out to capture flora or fauna at a time like this.

The newspaper illustrator's tone was grim as she went right on drawing and replied, "Neither. A time like this is the best time for me to try, if I'm to sketch a murderer from memory!"

The one who'd been crying looked up hopefully to ask, "Do you mean you can draw us a *picture* of that horrid monster who just shot poor Hiram?"

The professional with a pencil replied, "I'm not drawing this for anyone but the proper authorities and my paper, in that order. I think it might have been a Red Indian. I'm certain he wasn't made up as any *female* deity! I'll see about some copies for you ladies later."

So the next thing Phaedra knew both young widows were seated on her side of the coach, making helpful as well as dumb suggestions about the garish figure all three of them had just seen.

One of the Mormon girls—they were only related by marriage—felt those spiral designs on the villain's dusky hide had been tattoos. A member of her family had returned from a whaling cruise with some South Sea Island tattoos and she'd never forgotten that blue-black color, or the way some of the older Mormon women had carried on.

Phaedra said she drew things the way they looked to her and let others decide just what she'd seen. She explained how she'd been hired out of art school by a savvy art director because she could only draw things the way they looked and simply didn't understand that impressionistic manner the art critics were gushing about these days.

The *Illustrated London News* catered to a readership who

seldom visited fashionable art galleries and liked their news illustrated as close to photography as its roving quick-sketch artist was able to manage.

So by the time they rolled into the stage stop near the ford of the muddy La Plata, Phaedra Thorne had produced a penciled portrait of a naked killer in a kachina mask that the admiring Jehu and both widows declared a close-to-life likeness.

Phaedra modestly explained she meant to go over her penciling with ink and watercolors before turning it over to the authorities at the end of the line in Durango, Colorado.

The station manager, seated with them at a long plank table while they waited for their supper, could only take their word for the odd disguise at least one of the road agents had been wearing.

He suspected, and the others agreed after some reflection, that plain old crooks gussied up as Pueblos and Mexicans made way more sense than the real thing. For they were a good four hundred miles north of Old Mexico and a fair piece from any pueblos where you'd expect to meet up with a kachina, flesh or spiritual in form.

As a plump Ute woman came out of the kitchen to start serving them bread and beans, the station manager added, "When you *do* meet up with a real kachina it ain't sup-posed to shoot folk and run off with strongboxes. The Hopi, Zuni, and such hold six or seven such dances every year, with gents in masks like that one prancing all over with their bells and rattles. I can't say why. Neither white folk nor Injuns from other nations are allowed to join in. But I'm pretty sure nobody is supposed to get robbed or shot dead!"

The Jehu shrugged and said, "I told you to begin with I have no idea who jumped me when I reined in alone at Turner's Gap. I just done as they told me, in plain Amer-ican. The ones pretending to be greasers run off on foot with the strongbox. This wilder-looking cuss was the one

8

as shot Tom Cartier and Hiram Webber of Provo in the Utah Territory. I agree the loco way they was dressed was meant to confound us all. But I doubt they ever expected this little lady to be able to draw this good. So thanks to the way she got the rascal down on paper, tight as any tintype, they could be in more trouble than they planned on!''

As this was being said, a few miles west of Durango a whole lot of further complications were coming in by rail, wearing a crushed dark Stetson, a tobacco tweed suit, and a double-action Colt .44-40, riding cross-draw under the left tail of his frock coat. Deputy U.S. Marshal Custis Long of the Denver District Court carried his badge pinned in his billfold unless someone asked to see it. Longarm, as he was better known to friend and foe alike, wasn't looking to flash his badge or arrest anybody in Durango. He was on his way there to serve a warrant and transport a federal prisoner back to the jurisdiction of his own court.

After riding six or eight years for the Justice Department, Longarm wasn't expecting any trouble with his simple chore.

But then, in a world where there was never any trouble, the Justice Department wouldn't have needed riders like Longarm to begin with.

Chapter 2

Durango was a railroad town. Literally. Built on speculation in the Animas Valley by the Denver & Rio Grande Western to sell off some railroad-grant land, the still-modest county seat was surrounded by vacant city blocks they hoped to unload as the fair bottomland and marginal hill grazing west of the continental divide drew more settlers.

The newly incorporated La Plata County had a pro tem sheriff who'd be running for formal election come November. Such town law as there was need for was provided by the company police of the D&RGW. Crusher Cosgrove had been picked up drunk and disorderly by the railroad dicks, who'd noticed the federal flyers posted on the surly cuss before he'd sobered up and paid his fine.

Longarm was glad they still held vagrants, drunks, and such in that company jail handy to their railroad terminal. For the afternoon train he was getting off would be headed back to Denver as their night train just after sundown and he meant to be aboard it with his prisoner when it left. They were only running one train a day, so far, and the thought of a whole twenty-four hours doing nothing in Durango inspired a certain springiness to the lawman's walk as he made for the lockup in his low-heeled army boots.

As he strode inside with his federal warrant already out, a balding railroad dick with a sheepish smile told him, "We've been worried you might show up, Longarm. We wired your boss, Marshal Billy Vail, in the hope you hadn't left Denver yet. But I see you had."

Longarm smiled uncertainly down at the older man seated behind a big cheap desk and explained, "I had to leave Denver to get up here and take Crusher Cosgrove off your hands."

The railroad dick sighed and said, "You can't have him. Not right now, leastways. That's why we wired you not to come, see?"

To which Longarm replied, less friendly, "I'm afraid I don't see. You've been holding him, sobered up, on a city ordinance. This here federal warrant, signed by Judge Dickerson of the Denver District Court, demands the bastard's neck for the hangman's noose, save for some mere formalities in front of twelve men good and true. We got him cold on murder, rape, and stealing an army horse. So trot him out and let me haul him back to Denver aboard that same train I rode in on, damn it!"

The railroad dick shook his balding head and explained, "The mean bastard has the measles. The doc says he must have been feverish as well as drunk when he busted up that saloon the other night. But he never busted out in a rash until this morning. The doc says measles are still catching a week after the rash fades away and his rash has just commenced."

Longarm started to say something dumb. But he knew that while he, himself, was immune to most childhood vexations, there'd be no saying how many passengers a prisoner with measles in full flower might be able to infect aboard a night train with the windows shut.

The railroad dick said Crusher Cosgrove was being

treated for his rash and fever in an isolated cell, if Longarm wanted to visit with him.

Longarm growled, ''Never came to visit with the murderous son of a bitch. They sent me to fetch him for the judge and jury. How soon is that night train fixing to head back to Denver?''

When the railroad dick told him he had less than an hour to work with, Longarm swore and left without shaking hands or offering the cuss a smoke. Longarm was allowed to think for himself in the field because he tried to be thoughtful. He knew his boss, Marshal Vail, would likely want him to head directly back instead of wasting a whole week in the high country just to save some railroad fare. But older lawmen who sat down way more had feelings too. So Longarm decided he'd better wire the news about Crusher Cosgrove in and let old Billy Vail have the comfort of the final say.

The Western Union was as handy to the railroad terminal as all the other important parts of Durango. So it only took him a few minutes to get off a terse message, with an urgent request for a damned sudden answer. That left him time for the supper he'd missed aboard the fool freight and passenger coach combination. So he legged it on over to a chili parlor across from the tracks, watching his step.

It was cloudy in the west as the sun was setting, and the light was tricky enough for a country boy to step in horseshit if he failed to pay attention. But he did and so he strode into the chili parlor with clean boot heels, hoping to be back aboard that train before the street outside was really messy.

As he took a stool at the counter, the buxom Swedish gal serving a fair Mex menu said, ''Evening, Deputy Long. Do you think it will rain tonight?''

Longarm was trying to remember how he knew she was Swedish. He was sure he'd have remembered her if he'd ever known her in the biblical sense. Hoping she wouldn't

12

notice he didn't remember her name, he said it felt that way to him too and added, "Range all about could use some rain. I was noticing how brown the short-grass has got, considering how early in the summer it is. Could you serve me a rare steak under really hot chili, with my coffee black and double-action? I have some staying awake to manage tonight, no matter how things turn out."

The big blonde could. But she naturally asked what action a man of the world might have on his mind in a town like Durango. As she poured him some coffee while they waited for the old Mex gal in the back to sizzle his steak a mite she added, "It's not so bad when the herds are in town. But on a weeknight in early summer I'd as soon sling hash at that wide spot in the road south of Cheyenne, and I told you at the time what I thought of that job!"

The mousetrap snapped and he was once more back in that tiny trail town, at about this time of the year but later in the evening, waiting for another train.

He'd naturally glanced at her ring finger whilst he'd ordered. If she was spoken for she wasn't letting on. But long ago and farther away she'd discouraged a wayfaring stranger with a tale of impending marriage to a self-proclaimed cattle baron, or had it been a windmill salesman? Her name was Selma, he was almost sure, but a man spent many a lonely supper time flirting with a lonely waitress if he got around all that much.

As if he'd been rude enough to ask, she only waited until she was serving him his steak smothered in chili before she leaned across the counter to confide, "The louse never came back from Omaha, after all those promises! After I'd said no to you and heaps of boys almost as good-looking!"

Longarm didn't like to talk with his mouth full. So he had to stop, and he was hungry, as he replied, "I could have told you at the time that all men are beasts, Miss . . . Selma?"

She nodded and he continued, "I never did because, like

13

yourself, I was hoping in my heart of hearts he'd told you true when he gushed at you so romantic.''

She sighed and said, ''I remember. It would turn your head if you knew how often I've remembered that night when I turned down a famous lawman, for a sweet-talking liar who wasn't nearly as nice, once you left out promises to carry a girl off to his palace in the sky!''

Longarm didn't answer. He was never going to catch that night train if he didn't finish his damned supper, and a gal who served the same sort of grub to others ought to understand a man et in a hurry because he was in a hurry.

She let him eat in peace, pretending to buff her nails at the far end of the empty counter until it was time to pour him another cup and ask what he wanted for dessert.

He said, ''I might have time for a whole blamed pie, or no time at all. I'm waiting on a telegram from Denver. I'd best pay up and see if it's come in yet. It's been nice meeting up with you again, if they want me to catch that night train back.''

She looked mighty wistful as he left her a dime extra and departed to see if Billy Vail had wired yes or no. When he got to the Western Union Billy hadn't wired anything at all. They had no messages for him as, not far off, the engineer tolled the boarding bell of the one and only train out of Durango for a good twenty-four hours.

Longarm stepped out into the gathering darkness, smelling rain before morning for certain as he lit a three-for-a-nickel cheroot and muttered, ''Catch the damned train. The worst thing Billy can do is send you back for Cosgrove, and the son of a bitch won't be going nowhere for at least a week!''

But he somehow found himself drifting back across the street as the engineer tooted the whistle of the night train in a ready-to-roll manner. Blowing smoke out both nostrils like an angry bull, Longarm warned himself, ''You're playing the fool over a gal who's only sort of good-looking!

14

She's turned you down once already, and it looks like rain by quitting time! Do you really want to check into a hotel alone, soaking wet, with a hard-on, and spend another whole day up this way, with nothing to do but cuss yourself out for letting the same gal turn you down twice?''

But he kept on walking toward the chili parlor, knowing he'd cuss himself for missing his dessert and never finding out for certain if the lady had changed her mind or not.

She hadn't. It took him two slices of serviceberry pie before he could tell her, between other customers, how he'd been told to stay overnight in Durango after all.

She seemed so delighted by the notion he felt he owed it to her, as an old pal, to warn, "Of course, I could be leaving any time with my prisoner, come morning. I mean, it ain't as if I'll be up here all that long.''

She poured him more black coffee and got out a cup to serve herself some as well, murmuring, "I told you about all the times I've looked back to a night much like this one, Deputy Long?''

He allowed his friends called him Custis and added he'd never asked for such a tough name to remember.

So she wound up calling him Custis between customers until after nine and then all the way home to her hired cottage near the river. As they got there it began to rain. It was just a light drizzle, but it gave her the excuse to invite him in, at least until it was over, and it lasted long enough, as they sat on her davenport by candle-glow, for the two of them to cuddle and swap spit until she swore she'd kill him if he ran off and left her that "unfulfilled" a second time.

That was what some gals called feeling horny—unful-filled.

So he picked her up off the davenport, carried her into the one bedroom, and filled her good, once he'd undressed the two of them and had her on her brass bedstead with a pillow under her ample hips.

Selma gasped in mingled concern and delight as Long-arm parted the straw-colored thatch of her groin with his own excitement. When she moaned endearingly about the size of it, he smiled down at her to modestly reply, "Aw, I ain't hung all that much. You're just built as tight as a schoolgal with her legs crossed, no offense."

The big-boned but surprisingly small-built blonde enfolded his naked waist in her long lanky legs and hugged him closer to her big firm breasts as she demanded, "How often do you shove that banana up a schoolgirl, peel and all, you wicked thing?"

He said he had to admit it might have been smaller when he'd been a wicked schoolboy back in West-by-God-Virginia before the war. Then they were too busy to talk for a spell as he pounded on to glory.

He didn't ask why she was crying, once they'd stopped for a smoke in hopes of catching their second winds. Waitress gals who said no the first time were inclined to cry after they'd come at last.

So he just held her naked body against his own under the one sheet as he fumbled a cheroot from his nearby vest pocket, lit it one-handed, and offered her a puff as soon as he had it going good.

She took a deep drag, inhaling like a heavy-smoking man, and let it out with a mighty sigh before she said, "I'm sorry, Custis. I'm trying to be a big brave girl about all this. I know this means no more to you than playing with yourself, but . . ."

"That ain't true," he cut in. Then reaching his free hand down to pet her warm moist delta of Venus, he added, "Can't you tell even the helping hand of a friend don't feel as good as the real thing?"

She spread her big pale thighs wider as she moaned, "Do that some more. Harder. I love it, even when I don't have a friend to turn to. But I wasn't talking about the way it feels, Custis. It feels wonderful, no matter how you come.

16

But a woman can't help feeling emotional in other ways at times like this and . . . Oh, never mind, you'd never understand, you lovely animal!"

Longarm took the cheroot back, enjoyed a puff, and told her animals had emotions too. He said, "It's all right to fall in love with any lover while you're coming with him, honey. It's only natural to feel the only other human being who matters to you at such times is the only one who matters. I suspect what gets you gals in more trouble over no-good men is that a man can remember a woman is no-good once he's come in her. Ain't nobody ain't in real sincere love when they're really feeling full climax. They'd never admit it, but whores who sneer at kid trail herders are likely in love with them for as long as eight or ten seconds at a time, now and again."

She sighed and confessed, "When I first felt you sliding into me I felt sure I'd kill myself if you ever took it out. Now I only want to follow you to the ends of the earth and kill any other woman you ever look at. Do you think there's any cure for this condition, dear?"

He said he only knew one way to treat it. She said dog style was new to her and not really that romantic, until he'd pounded her awhile that way, his bare feet spread on her bedroom rug as he gripped a big hipbone in each hand to really slam it into her until her open mouth was drooling on the bedding. Her spine was arched to take all he had as deep as he could ram it, and she was sobbing over and over that she loved him, that she'd love him forever, and that she wanted to be his love slave and suffer every outrage to her groin that he had ever considered in his wildest dreams.

She seemed a little disappointed with a few of the wilder positions from that Hindu book he'd bought in a plain brown wrapper, down Yuma way. The Italo-Mexican gal he'd shared it with had found some of those Kama Sutra notions mighty stimulating. But, then, she'd been built

17

more supple, now that he studied on the two of them with renewed interest.

He figured, by the time he could ever catch a train out of Durango, he and good old Selma would both be about ready for a change of partners as well as position. But in the meantime it was a heap of fun to wear out his welcome by parting her mat as many ways as the two of them could come up with. So he did, they even got some sleep before morning, and it was fun to start all over in the sunshine streaking through her lace curtains as the day dawned bright and clear after all that scattered rain.

Selma knew better than to ask about their future after breakfast in bed. As he enjoyed the swell eggs she'd scrambled for him, Longarm resisted saying he'd likely be back up this way in a week or so, once Crusher Cosgrove was over the measles. She had to get back to work at her twelve-hours-a-day job. So he didn't know how on earth he'd ever pass away the time left over before he could catch that night train after sundown. He was still glad he'd missed the last one. Old Selma was still nice to look at after all that slap and tickle. He doubted it would kill him to spend another whole night with a buxom blonde who wanted to follow him to the ends of the earth. But, Jesus, a whole workday afternoon, doing nothing, in Durango?

Chapter 3

There was a telegram waiting for him when Longarm made it back to the Western Union near the terminal. As he read it Longarm had to admire the suspicious nature of his older boss. Old Billy said to get a second opinion. He pointed out that Crusher Cosgrove had grown up in a slum back east over thirty years ago. So how come a white man who'd done heaps of prison time as well had never caught the measles before Judge Dickerson had sent for him?

Longarm put the wire away and stepped out on the boardwalk to light a smoke and consider Billy Vail's notion. Longarm knew there were ways old jailbirds could manage fevers and rashes on demand. But he was going to have to put it delicate when he asked the local company police to let him call in an outside sawbones. And after he did, how was he to know an old con who could fool one doc couldn't fool another?

As he was shaking out the waterproof Mex match, a familiar voice hailed him by name and he turned to see one of the deputies he knew from the La Plata County Sheriff's Department.

Deputy Sheriff Kevin Malone's parents had fled the Great Potato Famine from County Clare. So he pronounced his last name "Maloon" but spoke as American in other ways as most gents raised west of the Big Muddy. He was way shorter as well as somewhat younger than Longarm, dressed in a finer suit with his German silver star pinned to a lapel and his S&W .38 packed under his coat in a shoulder holster, like he admired the rival railroad police around Durango.

Longarm could tell Malone had been talking with them as soon as he said, "We just heard you were in town, Uncle Sam. The coach from the Mormon Delta rolled in overdue last night, with upset survivors and tales of a mighty curious robbery. We're still arguing just who might have jurisdiction on that recent Indian Country to the west of the La Plata. It has to be at least partly federal and you're good with Indians. So we'd like you to posse up with us."

Longarm shook his head to reply, "I'd like to. Don't see how I can. I'm over this way on another chore and . . . You say that stage was robbed by *Indians*?"

"We're still working on that," Malone replied. "One of the lady passengers is a professional picture drawer from some big London newspaper. She's booked into the hotel just down the way by the train tracks. Have you got time to come see the picture she drew of one of the outlaws after he'd shot two men dead?"

Longarm glanced up at the morning sun and allowed he'd be proud to interview the survivors at least.

But as the two of them walked side by side toward the hotel he'd have spent the night in if he hadn't been so lucky, Malone told him the two widow women of one murdered Mormon were bunking across town with some kith or kin of the same persuasion.

Malone added, "You wouldn't get much out of either. I did my best. But it's tedious talking with two gals who talk at once and cry at the same time. Lem Redfern, the Jehu,

20

and that Miss Thorne who draws so good tell much the same tale of the robbery and both killings. Lem and the two Mormon gals agreed Miss Thorne's sketch of the peculiar-looking bastard captured his likeness exact.''

Longarm asked what looked so peculiar about the killer. Malone told him to wait until they got there and he could see for himself. Malone added, ''I ain't sure I believe the cuss really looked like that, myself.''

When they got to the nearby hotel they found two other deputies and a railroad dick in the taproom off the lobby with a shabbier coachman of, say, forty and a pretty little thing in a goofy hat and summer-weight calico dress. Longarm was glad he'd just torn off another piece with good old Selma about an hour before. It allowed him not to smile too goofy as he was introduced to the ravishing brunette. He knew her obvious poor eyesight made her stare at him like so through her horn-rimmed glasses. It still made him feel like kissing her.

But they only shook hands as Malone explained how great Longarm was with Indians. She led them all across the taproom to where her sketch pad and art kit sat on a table near the better light of one front window. She bade Longarm sit closer to the light. Then she sat down beside him and opened the protective cardboard cover of her pad.

Longarm stared soberly down at her more recently inked and washed rendering of what seemed mighty close to Matsop, the Hopi version of Dan Cupid. Longarm drily asked if the maple leaf the figure had on had been real or artificial.

Some of the other lawmen who'd asked earlier looked away. But Phaedra Thorne's tone was matter-of-fact as she replied, ''He was starkers, and rather virile about it. That's meant to be a *fig* leaf, and art students are supposed to disregard it.''

The Jehu, Lem Redfern, chimed in with, ''He was dark-skinned as an Indian, save for them dotty lines all over his bare hide.''

Longarm stared soberly down, careful about his tobacco ashes, as he softly replied, "That's the detail I'm having trouble with. They let me watch one of them *wimi* dances down to Black Mesa one time. I was asking a Hopi lady I knew there what was going on. I asked polite enough for her to explain more than they usually do. So I might know more about kachina notions than this outlaw gussied up Hopi style."

An older lawman standing by asked if Longarm was sure of the nation.

Longarm shook his head and said, "The mask is Hopi for certain. The kachinas or cloud people are supposed to look like the gods and ancestors of particular Indians. Matsop is the fertility spirit who helps Hopi ladies have big families. The kachina dancer standing in for him at a *wimi* only *gestures* at them, sort of forward, of course."

Phaedra Thorne said primly, "The bloke gesturing with those guns at us was certainly forward enough. But I thought a fig leaf might allow me to sign my name to this sketch. Aren't you as certain about my other details, Deputy Long?"

Longarm said his friends called him Custis and went on to explain to all of them, "That turtle-shell rattle looks kachina. Them trading post bells look kachina. Them curly dotted lines look all wrong for a kachina, flesh or cottonwood. Matsop and his fellow spooks usually get to wear more duds, and such skin as they expose is painted in solid colors. Sometimes you'll see a kachina dancer with handprints or some other simple design over his red, white, or black body paint. I've yet to spy a kachina with dotted lines over mostly bare hide. The most complexicated body paint I've seen at any *wimi* dances at any pueblo by any nation was that black and white prison striping, *broad* black and white stripes, worn by *koshares*, or clowns, not holy-rolling kachinas."

Phaedra Thorne said, "Maybe this odd bloke who robbed

our coach had no choice in the matter. One of the other ladies with me suggested all those dotted lines might be tattoos, and don't some of your Red Indians tattoo themselves, ah, Custis?"

One of the other lawmen exclaimed, "She's right! Some do! What about them Pawnee Picts, over Kansas way?"

Longarm made a wry face and said, "Mojave tattoo their chins, and some extinct Florida tribe used to tattoo themselves head to foot, albeit not in this curly corkscrew way. If we do assume the cuss was tattooed, and not just painted so strange, we're right back to what I've been trying to tell you. This ain't no picture of no Hopi kachina."

Lem Redfern snorted, "Hell, I could have told you all that. Sorry, Miss Thorne. What I meant was that the others with him, running off with our strongbox whilst he was gunning poor Tom Cartier and that Mormon elder, were dressed like Mexicans and yelling at me in plain American to toss the box down to them. Ain't it obvious to one and all that all three of the rascals were *disguised* for the occasion?"

Longarm smiled thinly and agreed, "I doubt they'd be gussied up as two Mexicans and a Hopi kachina if they rode in right now, which they might have by now."

He pointed at Phaedra's sketch, careful not to touch the paper, as he continued, "I'll have to ask. But there can't be a full dozen known outlaws on this continent, tattooed chin to toe with such fancy designs. So if any of you *were* such a wonder, and you aimed to hold up a stagecoach wearing any sort of mask, would you expose your unusual bare hide below said mask?"

Kevin Malone whistled thoughtfully and said, "I told you gents when I went to fetch him that this old boy knows his onions. I vote for this cuss in the picture being a white man or mayhaps a Mex who only *drew* them lines all over his fool self with, say, a pen and ink."

There came a murmur of agreement. Longarm started to

disagree, but shrugged and decided, "Makes more sense than some tattooed wonder anxious for everyone to know he'd left show business to rob stagecoaches. I've noticed how greenhorns playing Indian tend to mess up the details in dumb ways. There's this one famous explorer who had his fool self photographed in a fringed deerskin shirt with Siksika quillwork. I reckon nobody told him, when they were making him an honorary member of the Blackfoot Nation, that they'd just sold him a squaw's outfit."

Phaedra Thorne smiled dubiously and quietly asked, "Isn't it an insult to call a Red Indian woman a *squaw*?"

Longarm calmly answered, "Depends on her nation. The Lakota word for woman sounds more like *winyan* or *weyah*, depending on her band. You call a Na-déné gal an *asdza* if you aim to be polite, and in Ute or Ho she'd be a *wuhti*. But Arapaho, Cheyenne, Blackfoot, and such are Algonquin speakers who say *esquah*—squaw—or something close."

Kevin Malone chuckled and said, "Don't argue with him. He knows!"

Phaedra smiled sheepishly and said, "I stand corrected, and I've noticed those African Zulu shields some Sioux seem to be carrying in one version of Custer's Last Stand. What if that bloke in the Hopi Indian mask mixed up tribal decorations from completely different cultures? One of those Mormon girls thought the killer's tattoos might have been a South Sea Island design."

Longarm peered closer, ran some library books through his mind as if they'd been reward posters, and decided, "By Jimmy, *that's* where I've seen such whirly-curly dotted lines! In an illustrated book about whaling in the South Seas by Mr. Herman Melville. Do any of you recall the name and nation of that South Sea Islander who signed aboard with Captain Ahab to go after Moby Dick?"

The more traveled English girl blinked at him to blurt, "No, but by George you've got it! I've seen not only pho-

24

tographs but dried heads in the British Museum, and the New Zealand native Maoris are tattooed exactly like this chap! But why has it taken me this long to see that?''

Longarm told her gently, ''You wasn't expecting to meet up with South Sea Island natives on the Colorado Plateau, no offense. We tend to see what we're expecting to see, Miss Phaedra. Any lawman can tell you how often you wind up with three descriptions out of two witnesses. Most of us go through life barely looking but sure we're seeing things the way they ought to be. That other artist who handed out Zulu battle gear at the Battle of Little Big Horn never thought too hard about it as he decided a savage was a savage and never looked up Lakota medicine shields. So what if this cuss you captured on paper just gussied his fool self up from a scattering of travel books he begged, borrowed, or stole?''

Kevin Malone proved he was worth his salt by volunteering, ''It might be worth asking all around about looted libraries, then!''

Longarm smiled thinly and replied, ''Anyone can see this cold trail has to be followed mostly on paper now. If I were you I'd wire far and wide about tattooed men who've recently run away from a circus, or a prison too. The Bureau of Indian Affairs might have something on stolen kachina masks. Most such masks are just whipped up for the one occasion. But Matsop's mask is *mon kachina*, or church property, that ordinary folk, red or white, ain't allowed to mess with. The theft of a mon kachina mask would occasion more excitement amongst the Hopi than a bank robbery in downtown Denver might amongst us.''

Malone said he'd send a mess of wires before they rode. Then he said, ''We mean to ride, as soon as all the others we've sent word to ride in to join us by high noon. How come you consider it such a cold trail, Longarm? It was only late yesterday afternoon, not more than twenty miles off when you count all the bends in the wagon trace!''

Longarm said, "It rained last night. More than once. I sort of doubt the robbers rode far dressed as two Mexicans and a kachina. We don't know which way they rode, or on what, but they were likely a good ways east or west, if it wasn't north or south, when those raindrops come out of the west to pitty-pat all their hoof marks, heel marks, or mayhaps roller skate marks away."

He moved to open the casement window beside him and get rid of his smoked-down cheroot as he grumbled, "You don't trail outlaws with a good lead on you by sniffing at the ground like a bloodhound for sign that ain't there. You figure out who they might have been and which way they might have gone."

He began to fieldstrip the cheroot into shredded tobacco that could be disposed of by the breezes along the walk out front as Lem, the Jehu, flatly stated, "They never rid, walked, or roller-skated this way. Miss Phaedra, me, and heaps of others would have spotted anybody crossing the river at the ford. There's no better place to cross, for miles up or down the banks. The armed buckboard crew we sent to fetch them two dead bodies never saw so much as distant dust betwixt the La Plata relay station and said bodies neither!"

The railroad dick opined, "I'd never ride east or west along the trail of any stage I'd just robbed. I'd want to get out of Colorado jurisdiction, pronto. So I'd beeline south, and where does that take us?"

"Indian Country," said an older sheriff's deputy with the tanned face of a man who'd ridden some. He declared as firmly, "We're only a few hours ride from the South Ute Strip, with Navaho beyond, as far south as I'd ever want to ride dressed up Hopi or Mex. Of course, they could be headed for Mesa Verde, where nobody lives at all these days."

Phaedra Thorne asked, "Doesn't Mesa Verde mean Green Table in Spanish?"

26

The old-timer nodded and replied, "That's what it looks like, ma'am, eighty-odd square miles of tableland, covered by a green tablecloth of juniper and pinyon, with smaller mesas, just as high, all around."

The English girl calculated in her head and decided, "I say, that adds up to a green table indeed!"

"Almost four times the size of that Manhattan Island back east," the old-timer replied. "Used to be heaps of cliff dwelling Indians, yonder. Half the canyons they still haunt ain't been explored as yet. Navaho and Ute steer clear of the Mesa Verde. But most all them cliff dwelling have water as well as firewood and fodder handy."

Kevin Malone nodded eagerly and declared, "That sounds like a swell part of this old world to start hunting. Are you with us, Longarm?"

Before Longarm could answer a bullet crashed through the casement he'd been closing. The crown and broad brim of his Stetson caught a heap of the shattered glass as the hot lead almost parted his hair. Then he shoved the startled Phaedra Thorne off the far end of the bench they'd been sharing and threw himself atop her as another shot showered them with more busted glass.

Kevin Malone made the deputies shooting back hold their fire before their wild fusillade could do too much damage to downtown Durango. In the ringing silence that ensued Longarm rolled off the English girl, his own .44-40 in hand. He told her he was sorry if he'd scared her. She dimpled up at him to reply it had been the sod outside who'd had her worried.

Malone asked Longarm who the sniper could have been out to get.

Longarm drily replied, "I'll ask him when we catch him. It seems obvious we won't have to ride clean to Mesa Verde after the cuss!"

Chapter 4

Before high noon scores of gents with other business in Durango that morning had given convincing accounts of where they'd been at the time some other son of a bitch must have fired on an assemblage of lawmen. More than one who looked Indian or Mex had been politely but firmly required to unbutton his damned shirt.

Longarm spent most of that time sending wires far and wide. He'd seldom had anyone spitting and whittling near the scene of recent gunplay own up to the same.

He knew they had the whole afternoon to work with, once those posse recruits coming in from all directions assembled out front of the sheriff's office up the street. For there was no way their wild-shooting secret enemy could have left town afoot or astride, and the one daily train wasn't due in or out for hours.

Lem Redfern had explained how his stage line meshed with the one train over the continental divide. They got their passengers, mail, and cargo into Durango early in the evening so's eastbound travelers could catch the night train. A fresh crew carried day trainers west to Utah Territory by way of the canyon country, by night coach.

Lem couldn't rightly say how much had been in that strongbox the oddly disguised road agents had taken from him. He said such boxes were put aboard padlocked at either end of the line. He said, just guessing, Mormon bankers liked to take the U.S. Treasury up on what was printed on its paper money. U.S. silver certificates allowed a paper dollar bill could be exchanged on demand for its value in silver, and they coined solid silver dollars at the Denver Mint. That meant the robbers had carried off more money in the form of paper than two men might have managed if the box had been filled with bullion. Longarm set such estimates on the back of the stove for the time being. The crooks had interfered with the U.S. Mails on unsettled open range, making their dirty deeds federal, as far as Longarm could see. He didn't want to wade in any deeper before old Billy Vail agreed with him, unless he had to. It still wasn't clear whether those bullets through the taproom window had been meant for him or most anyone else in the room. When you stood across the way from the hotel you could see well into the taproom at long pistol range, bless the way most pistols carried high.

When he got back to the hotel from the Western Union, that English gal from London had gone up to her hired room, according to the only deputies left in the taproom. Neither knew why and suggested Longarm have a drink with them at the bar.

He did, not learning anything new from them or having anything to tell them before he got some answers to his wired questions. Then, a man of the world planning his moves in advance on his feet, Longarm excused himself from the boys bellied up to the bar and headed for that chili parlor Selma Larsson worked at. He knew they served better grub. Just as he'd known better than to invite that newspaper gal to join him there for the same.

It was still a tad early in the day for noon diners. So Longarm found the buxom blonde cleaning the counter as the only other eater left. Their cook was in the back. So they were free to talk private as he took a stool, and he asked right off what she'd been crying about.

Selma leaned over the counter to kiss him, confiding, "I've been beside myself with worry over you, Custis! They told me hours ago that someone had taken a shot at you, and you never came by to tell me you were still alive! I had to ask and ask before I knew they'd missed you and that stuck-up English girl!"

Longarm said, "Aw, Miss Phaedra ain't all that stuck-up. They all talk like that. She's just passing through town with her drawing pad. She was aboard that coach they robbed late yesterday, and you should have seen the swell picture she drew us of one of the road agents."

He brought her up-to-date as she served him chili over cob-cured ham, leaving out how nice Phaedra Thorne smelled up close. Selma had already heard her dark-haired rival was pretty, she said.

Longarm chuckled wryly and declared, "Miss Ellen Terry, the English actress, is as pretty, and as likely to set on my knee when you ain't looking. I told you Miss Phaedra works for that *Illustrated London News*, drawing pictures of us wild and wooly Westerners for the same. She'll doubtless be leaving tonight aboard that night train. The railroad dicks stuck up for her when the sheriff's men suggested we hold her as a material witness. The D&RGW don't make money off fares they can't carry over the mountains and, like I told 'em at the same time, them three road agents are likely long gone. They got the money and a good start, with miles and miles of nothing but miles and miles to ride into. Did we posse up right now, they'd be fifty miles off or better by the time we cut their trail, if we could read any sign after that rain we had last night."

Selma poured his second coffee as she sort of purred she was glad he wouldn't be riding off after outlaws. Then, being a woman, she had to sweetly ask if he might be riding back to Denver on that same night train, with that pretty Miss Thorne.

He purred back, "I doubt it. When I told you this morning I was through here in Durango for the time being, I hadn't heard tell of kachina dancers interfering with the U.S. Mails. Neither had my boss in Denver, Marshal Vail. So I reckon I'll be helping you close up this evening after all."

"Is that all I am to you, a handy place to hang your hat whilst you shoot your wad?" she suddenly blazed, inspiring the fat Mex gal to peer around the doorjamb, poker-faced.

Some women were like that. Longarm quietly sipped some coffee while he tried to think up a nice way to tell a buxom blonde to take her old ring-dang-doo home alone, for all he cared.

She seemed to read his mind. Some women were like that too. She sobbed, "I didn't mean that, darling! Of course I want you to shoot your wad in me some more! It's just that you have me so mixed up with your on-again, off-again ways and . . . Oh, I don't know what I mean."

Longarm gently murmured, "That's all right. I do. I ought to be horsewhipped for even talking to ladies decent as yourself, Selma. I try to level with you all. I ain't sure why that only seems to mix you up. Some kindly French sage once wrote that women expect the men they kiss to change, whilst men expect the sweet gals they kiss to stay just the same, leading both to wind up disappointed as all get-out."

She laughed despite herself and said they'd likely be closing late that night, because of all the posse riders in off the surrounding range. He would have kissed her some more had not a couple of hands strode in about then to order their own grub.

He allowed he'd see Selma later and headed back to the hotel, knowing the joint operations of the town and county law had settled on that taproom as Headquarters Pro Tem.

31

He found Phaedra Thorne there as well, sort of holding court at that same table with her sketch pad. She'd already sketched old Lem Redfern and a couple of senior sheriff's deputies for her newspaper. Longarm had to allow she'd drawn them close to the way they looked.

She invited Longarm to pose as well, explaining she meant to sell his likeness to London as a famous frontier sheriff.

He smiled wearily and replied, "I ain't no sheriff, Miss Phaedra. I'm a deputy U.S. marshal, and I ain't sure I'll have any connection with your illustrated stickup story unless they wire back that I'm to horn in."

Deputy Malone came over from the bar, saying, "You have to take command of the posse out in the field, Longarm."

Malone winked down at the English girl to add, "He's trying to act modest, ma'am. But everybody knows he's the best white tracker born of mortal woman!"

Longarm muttered, "Aw, mush!" as Phaedra Thorne commanded he sit down across from her.

He hesitated. Then he did. For he knew for a fact what he looked like. But he wasn't sure how tight she could draw. Those other quick sketches looked good enough at first glance. But, thinking back, he recalled slips of the pen or engraving tool that had caused a heap more trouble than no picture at all might have.

She asked him to take off his hat. As he set his Stetson on the table between them, he asked how come the *Illustrated London News* was still using line drawings instead of the new photo-engraving process invented by Mr. Ben Day.

She calmly replied, her pencil wagging like a pup's tail, that the Ben Day process was patented to begin with and that quick sketching would always have slow photography beat when it came to illustrating anything at all exiting.

She said, "They did take dreadfully still photographs of

our lads in the Crimea, back in '54. But to show our Light Brigade in *action* required work like mine, combining memory and imagination!''

Just how much imagination she'd used on that killer kachina was the question before the house. So he shut up and let her draw away to her heart's content and, when she'd finished, he had to allow her drawing of him was close to what he saw in the mirror every time he shaved his fool face.

She told him she'd make sure he got a ''proof'' or practice copy of the engraving they'd make of her pencil sketch. He said he'd get it if they sent it to the federal building in Denver. Then he asked if they had good engravers working for the *Illustrated London News*.

When she allowed they did, and asked why he was worried about it, Longarm explained, ''Back in the sixties a woodcut was circulated with a likeness said to be that of Black Jack Slade. It didn't look nothing like him. Black Jack was a mean drunk who could whistle and wittle if he wasn't required to do both at the same time. But that woodcut that looked like somebody else entire allowed him to live close to ten more years after shooting up Fort Halleck and riding off with a federal warrant out on him.''

Deputy Malone said, ''I remember hearing about Black Jack Slade and them Montana Vigilantes a spell back. They say he was an overseer for the Overland Stage Line who went bad and . . . Lord have mercy! Might you be suspecting Lem Redfern or someone he works for?''

Longarm was just as glad Redfern wasn't there. But he still said, ''That would work better if Miss Phaedra, here, hadn't seen such an odd road agent and drawn his picture, with other witnesses backing up her fine pencil work. They never proved Black Jack Slade robbed Overland when he was working for them. They fired him for being a mighty mean drunk after he tortured another Overland man, Jules Bene, to death. I was only pointing out how a poor likeness of a wanted killer can be a whole lot worse than no likeness at all.''

Smiling across the table at the myopic brunette, Longarm went on, ''Thanks to how close Miss Phaedra, here, draws faces I'm more familiar with, I'm buying that killer ka-china, save for the fig leaf, and may as well take Lem's word on the ones dressed Mex. Like Black Jack said at the time he was accused of stealing from Overland, it ain't as easy as all that to steal from the folk you work for. You're always the first one everyone suspects. Where is old Lem, right now, by the way?''

A railroad dick volunteered, ''Western Union, trying to recruit a new shotgun messenger. It's his turn to drive west this evening. He has to carry silver dollars back with him, after dark. Last I'd heard, he was hoping for a laid-off mining company guard, coming in from the east slope aboard the afternoon train.''

Longarm said that sounded fair, bought a round of drinks to make up for the free ones he'd been enjoying, and ex-cused himself to head over to the Western Union as well.

When he got there Lem Redfern had been there and left. Billy Vail had wired he was to use his own judgment, for now. Vail's wire added they'd be digging through the wanted flyer files in Denver as well.

The friendly telegraph clerk knew everyone of any im-portance in Durango. So Longarm asked him to name a sawbones who wasn't working for the railroad. The West-ern Union reeled off more than one. When he got to a sawbones of good rep who treated schoolkids for their childish agues, Longarm said that was just the sort of sec-ond opinion he was looking for.

He wrote down the name in his notebook and scouted the silver-haired and skinny Doc Burnett up, just short of supper time, as he was closing his clinic for the day.

The Durango baby doctor said he'd be proud to help the federal government out. So they drove down to the town lockup in the doc's one-horse shay and asked to see Crusher Cosgrove, out back.

The burly killer allowed he felt sort of wobble-kneed but better than he had the day before. Doc Burnett made him stick out his tongue and take off his shirt. Then he told Longarm, "Measles. Pure and simple. No evidence of laundry soap or brick massage as far as I can tell. He could make it to Denver with no danger to himself now. But he'll be contagious for at least another ten days at the least. I'd like another look at him before you expose the general public to this patient."

So Longarm told Crusher he was sorry he'd suspected him of faking and left him some cheroots and matches for later.

He shook with the doc out front and let the older man drive home alone. He returned to that taproom to find Phaedra Thorne seated at another table with her sketch pad and a stein of ginger beer.

She said Deputy Malone and the others had told those posse riders to go home for supper and allowed that was where they'd be going as well, once they tidied up after hasty planning. By late afternoon it had seemed obvious to one and all that at least one of those road agents had to be lurking way closer than the scene of that robbery.

Longarm said he meant to be over by the tracks whilst that train from Denver rolled in and rolled out. He said he'd be proud to tote her baggage on over, if she meant to catch the night train east.

She said she didn't, explaining, "My editors would never forgive me if I just walked away from a story as colorful as this one!"

He asked what she found so colorful and she insisted killer kachinas robbing stagecoaches would seem colorful enough in London Town.

Meanwhile, she said, she was getting hungry and wasn't it almost suppertime by now?

He allowed it was and suggested she ask her room clerk if they'd throw in dining room fare with the room she'd hired upstairs. Then he got out of there with an awkward remark about meeting that train.

He was hungry, himself, when the damned train rolled in with only a few passengers, a heap of freight, and that silver bullion meant for those suspicious settlers in the Mormon Delta. Nobody tried to rob Lem Redfern as he and his new shotgun messenger from Denver took it off the railroad's hands. Longarm walked them over to the stage terminal to make sure and waved them off as they headed west into the sunset with some other Mormons off the train.

Then he headed for the chili parlor for his supper, with Selma Larsson planned for a late dessert. But when he got there he found a short plump redhead behind the counter instead.

He took the same stool and ordered steak and potatoes with his chili for a change. He waited until he'd been served and the redhead wasn't busy before he quietly asked if this was old Selma's night off.

The plump and plainer waitress answered, just as casually, that she was the owner's wife and that Selma had asked for the night off because her old true love from Omaha had caught up with her at last.

Longarm wasn't too surprised to hear more than he cared to about a cattleman who'd allowed he might be back from Omaha, once he'd seen about some stock sales there.

The son of a bitch reminded Longarm of himself. And it was way too late now to ask Miss Phaedra Thorne of the *Illustrated London News* if she'd care to sup with him that evening.

Chapter 5

The next morning, after a lonesome but otherwise comfortable night in a hired bed above that taproom, Longarm ambled back to the Western Union, reflecting that once they had that newfangled telephone of Mr. Bell strung right, a lawman in the field would doubtless be able to stay in touch with his home office a whole lot better.

As it was, the telegraph had writing beat and, as he'd hoped, they'd wired him a night letter, sent at lower rates during slack business along the cross-country wires. Billy Vail had sent him a considerable message after ordering old Henry, their prissy file clerk and typewriter player, to dig through those backdated wanted flyers as requested.

As long as he was there, Longarm wired Henry for a rundown on that new shotgun messenger he'd met the night before. Dick Lloyd, as he'd styled himself, had said he was licensed as a private gun by the state of Colorado. That would be easy for Henry to find out about, and such suspicions had paid off in the past. Albeit Lloyd's whereabouts at both the time of that robbery west of the La Plata and the gunplay here in Durango seemed without question and let him off on both counts.

Having somehow lost his taste for chili up this way, Longarm had breakfast at the hotel. It wasn't so bad, and it did go with the hire of the bed upstairs, on the American Plan.

He was fixing to leave when Phaedra Thorne came into the hotel dining room, dressed for riding, if you were riding after foxes, sidesaddle. She asked him where he was headed. He said he had a line on a tattooed South Sea Island boy gone wrong and that he was headed up to the sheriff's office to fill them in on the cuss.

He added, "Half-breed named Seth Cooper, when they writ it in the mission birth registry. You were on the money about him being tattooed New Zealand Maori style by his mother's kin. I was close-but-no-cigar about him signing aboard a Yankee whaler. He jumped ship in Frisco when his clipper from Down Under docked there. Why don't you have a good breakfast and we'll talk about it some more later?"

She told him firmly she was on her way to the sheriff's office with him and bade him wait while she fetched her sketch pad.

Then she scampered off in her dinky derby and black riding habit before he could tell her he was in a hurry. So he had to wait, but it didn't take her long. Phaedra Thorne was fast on her feet as well as imperious.

He walked them up the shady side of the street, with him on the outside betwixt her and Selma's chili parlor. He couldn't tell from across the way whether Selma had come to work that morning or not. He had a pretty clear picture of how that other son of a bitch had been served his own breakfast.

Deputy Malone came out on the walk in front of the sheriff's to say howdy to them, tugging his hat brim at their visitor from London as he took a break from questioning a suspect inside about some missing cows. Longarm agreed they might find the drugstore across the way a quieter place to converse after Malone pointed out they had a soda fountain.

The three of them crossed over, sat down at a bitty marble table near the window, and ordered three ginger beers. Malone said it was possible to have one's soft drinks needled with medicinal alcohol. Longarm and the English gal agreed it was a tad early in the day to start drinking that serious. Malone told them to speak for themselves and told the old druggist he'd have his soda pop with "The Curse of the Irish."

As they were waiting, Longarm told them both, "Seth Cooper from North Island, New Zealand, has been working as a bouncer along the Barbary Coast on Frisco Bay for better than ten years now. He spoke fair English when he jumped ship there, and they say he talks better American now. He was almost as well known as Frisco's old Emperor Norton, speaking of British subjects acting crazy by the Frisco Bay."

Phaedra brightened and said she'd heard about the Emperor Norton, Ruler of the United States and Protector of Mexico. Malone asked why they were talking about a South Sea Island bouncer in the past tense.

As the druggist placed their cold glasses on the marble table for the three of them, Longarm explained, "Cooper ain't been in Frisco for some time. He took part in another robbery out that way. Stopped one of the Banning stagecoaches down the coast a piece and gunned two passengers that time. He can't be very bright. He had a bandanna over the bottom half of his face. But when they tattoo you Maori style they tattoo thorough, and how many road agents have both dotted and solid lines all over their foreheads?"

Malone sipped some spiked soda pop and declared, "He must have been drunk."

Phaedra gasped, "You mean he was recognized by his victims in spite of his attempt to mask himself?"

Longarm nodded soberly and declared, "You're both

right. Cooper robbed the Banning stage because he was broke. They kept firing him from one place after another because he was inclined to bounce paying customers who hadn't done anything after he'd had a few drinks on the house. The California lawmen messed up by asking around the Frisco waterfront for a gent with no fixed address. So guess where he turns up next.''

Malone said firmly, ''Not here in La Plata County. Country folk gossip a mite about mean drunks tattooed head to toe like an infernal South Sea Island man-eater!''

Longarm nodded and said, ''They noticed that around the Great Salt Lake, even before he beat a man to death in a hobo jungle near Ogden. He robbed a post office and stole a horse on his way south through the Mormon Delta. The post office robbery made him a federal want.''

Phaedra Thorne asked if she was correct in assuming the Mormon Delta had to be the long narrow strip of irrigated farmlands between the foothills of the western slope and the arid sagebrush country further out. Longarm nodded and said, ''He was spotted and reported more than once, making his way south. But all this took place over a month ago. So by now he should have made it all the way to . . . Where would you hide out if you were covered hairline to toe with Maori tattooing, Malone?''

The county lawman grimaced and decided, ''Back to New Zealand, where I wouldn't be on the run with every man's hand raised against me. He can't hope to pass as any sort of gent who *belongs* in these parts. You just saw how unconvincing he was as an Indian, and I can't see him getting by as either Anglo or Mex.''

The English girl swallowed a sip of ginger beer and said, ''He had *me* convinced he was some sort of Red Indian, at first. But I've been thinking about what you said about those kachina dancers, Custis. You said they danced in clothes and body paint as well as those grotesque masks. So wouldn't it have made more sense for this Maori bloke to dress a bit warmer and paint himself one solid color if he wanted us to think we were being attacked by Red Indians?''

Longarm swallowed some of his own cooling drink, ginger beer having more taste to it than the more popular ginger ale, and decided, ''None of that playacting makes much sense when you consider all the effort. Frank and Jesse got away clean after that Northfield raid by peeling off the long canvas dusters they'd worn over their regular duds. It don't take a college degree to cover a tattooed head entire with a feed sack, and we know his two pals did that. So maybe he was *proud* of all them tribal tattoos. They likely mean something on his mamma's side, and he must have gone through a lot of pain in his boyhood while they were decorating him so thorough.''

The commercial artist shrugged and said, ''I've heard it pays to advertise, but really . . .''

Deputy Malone said, ''No offense, ma'am, but feminine intuition will be the death of the drinking man yet. You ladies imagine there's some logic you can follow to the mind of a drunk. But few drunks can tell you why they come up with such grand inspirations after a dozen or so, and you just heard Longarm tell us this Cooper breed is a known drunk with homicidal tendencies. I doubt he could tell us, if he was sitting here drinking ginger beer with us, why he thought stopping your coach disguised as a Hopi love god made sense!''

The county lawman finished his spiked refreshments, wisely refrained from ordering a second, and asked Longarm, ''Where do you think they headed afterwards? We do know the Mesa Verde ain't far.''

Longarm asked, ''To what end? Road agents don't ride off with a box of *dinero* just to bury it like pirates. I doubt pirates did that, half as much as some say. Gents who follow the owlhoot trail instead of an honest trade steal money to spend the same, and there's nowhere to buy a drink or dance the fandango around the Mesa Verde.''

The English girl said thoughtfully, "I remember we talked about that area and all those cliff dwellings before, Custis. So might not a gang of desperados hide out in such a remote maze of canyons until their trail, as you Americans say, goes bad?''

Longarm smiled, not unkindly, and said, "That's cold, Miss Phaedra. A trail goes cold, not bad. You're right about a maze of canyons over by the Mesa Verde, though. Half of 'em have yet to be explored, and thanks to that recent rain they've all been scoured smooth by running water. You get them canyons because water runs that way after a rain out this way. We could ask the U.S. Cav to tag along—few Indians would care to—and it would still take us all summer to explore even half of the Mesa Verde. There'd be eighty square miles of dense forest on top to poke through, after you'd satisfied yourself nobody was hiding out in any of them canyons, with or without cliff dwellings and bat caves to complexicate things.''

Malone said, "I follow your drift. But I'm still dead certain it couldn't have been a tattooed wonder shooting at us from across the street just yesterday. So where's this Cooper at if he's neither in these parts or them Mesa Verde parts?''

Longarm sighed and said, "I never said he couldn't be hither or yonder. I said he's hiding from us, wherever he may be. Nobody gave any of us even a fuzzy description of that shootist here in Durango, and we don't even know who the intended target might have been. We'd be running in even bigger circles atop the Mesa Verde, for all the good it might do. We don't *know* where those road agents went, after that robbery west of the La Plata. We don't *know* where the one who shot at us yesterday ducked, here in Durango. It's been my experience that when you just don't know where to look, you sit tight and wait for a bright notion on your part or a dumb move on their part to set you to rights."

Malone agreed that made sense and went back across the street to help his pals question those suspected stock thieves some more. When Phaedra asked Longarm how you went about questioning such suspects, he suggested it might be best if neither of them asked.

As he escorted her back to their hotel she wanted to know if he meant to question that New Zealand breed as thoroughly. Longarm shook his head and replied, "My boss wouldn't approve, and I'd rather feel sure I was getting the truth. Twenty old ladies in a town they called Salem confessed to flying about on broomsticks after they were yelled at and beat up a mite. You don't have to slap a tattooed man at all to prove he's covered with tattoos. So once we catch him it won't matter what he has to say about the bloody trail he's left from the Frisco Bay to the Colorado Plateau. You and a heap of other witnesses have already put the noose around his tattooed neck. It's tougher to get stock thieves to confess. The unfortunates across the way won't end up in prison unless the law recovers the stock, or at least one hide with the right brand on the same."

Back at the hotel, it was too early for either to suggest dinner. But when she awkwardly remarked she'd never managed to have breakfast, he grabbed the chance to escort her back to the hotel dining room, sit her down, and allow he'd have some coffee and mince pie as he sat down to keep her company.

The English gal had a healthy appetite for such a bitty thing, or else she was in no great hurry to get up from the table. Longarm had more coffee and some peach cobbler on top of his mince pie as they got to know one another better.

But there was no way to get to know a lady in the biblical sense on such short notice, albeit his hunting instincts told him she might be lonesome at night too. He found it easy enough to undress a gal in such a tailored riding habit with his own eyes. Even allowing for whalebone and stays, Phaedra Thorne hourglassed mighty nice betwixt her trim hips and healthy lung capacity.

They dawdled and nibbled well into the noon dinner hour and beyond as they both strove not to suggest they were done. For once they got up from the table there was no decent place he could ask her to go with him, unescorted. Young ladies of her generation and class just didn't "see" men they had no "understanding" with, and they'd both understand what he was asking if he invited her up to his hotel room. The taproom next door was almost as bad, if she went drinking there alone with him. The lawmen assembled all around her and her sketch pad the day before had been the exception to the rule that hotel taprooms were designed for men to drink in. She'd confided early on in the dining room how she'd been forced to turn in early and restless the night before when they'd warned her unescorted ladies weren't supposed to lounge about downstairs.

A walk around the block to settle their innards was the best he could come up with. From the way she took him up on the notion he was sure she wasn't ready to go back up to her room, alone, either. But he knew they were both doomed to long lonesome afternoons, if they strolled thrice around the damned block.

But they'd barely explored the shadier back street when they were saved, coming back to Main Street, by the sounds of whip cracks and yelling, over by the stage line's terminal and ticket office.

Joining the crowd as everyone in town seemed to converge on the buckboard and team out front, Longarm spied a railroad dick headed the other way and stopped him to ask what was going on.

The railroad dick said, "They done it again. Same stretch of the stage route west of the river! Lemme go! I got to

44

wire our Denver office the money we transported for them is still safe.''

But Longarm hung on to his sleeve, insisting, ''How can the money be safe if they've robbed the stage a second time?''

The railroad dick insisted, ''Let go my arm. I never said they robbed the stage. I meant they *tried* again! This time the coach was rolling down the grade, fast, when that same lunatic in that Indian outfit jumped out on the trail at 'em. Lem Redfern cracked his whip and that new shotgun messenger, Lloyd, put a load of number nine buck in the rascal in passing!''

Longarm whistled and asked if they'd killed the outlaw. The other lawman broke free, saying, ''Everybody lit out without looking back. So it's tough to say.''

Then he was gone, and Longarm and the girl moved on to meet Deputy Malone and some other local lawmen, grinning wolfishly. When Longarm allowed they'd heard, Malone said, ''We're fixing to ride. Last night was clear and dry. Them road agents lit out over fresh damp range and the tracking should be easier than usual. Are you riding with us?''

Longarm said he was, provided someone loaned him a horse, saddle, and saddle gun.

Phaedra Thorne said she was riding with them. Longarm started to tell her she couldn't. Then he wondered why any man would want to say a stupid thing like that.

Chapter 6

Malone was in charge whilst his boss sheriff was up in Silverton, kissing babies with a view to the first time the voters had anything to say about him, come November. So it was easier than it might have been for Longarm to talk some sense about posse riding across rugged country. He got Malone to agree it would take less time to posse up, and said posse would have a better chance against no more than a half dozen outlaws, if they whittled it down to no more than a dozen good riders on decent mounts, raising way less dust as they rode way faster than your usual mounted mob.

The sheriff's tack room had many a good saddle to go with all the swell riding stock in the corral out back. So Longarm allowed he'd be obliged if they'd select him some decent trail stock while he got his notes in better order. For next to riding fast, there was nothing like having some idea of where you might be going and what might be going on.

The two young stock handlers who'd driven in with the news from the station at the La Plata ford were sort of holding court in the combined coach terminal and ticket office when Longarm caught up with them, his notebook and stub pencil handy. A town lawman who'd been jawing with the young white boy and slightly older breed told everyone else to let Longarm question the suspects right.

Longarm smiled at the two scared-looking wranglers and perched one hip on the corner of a desk, saying, "Nobody here's a suspect, yet. But I am a mite puzzled about some details you boys can doubtless explain."

The breed hunkered down, his back to one wall, but the white boy remained standing, shifting his weight like he had to piss, as Longarm asked how come it had taken them so long to drive into town with the news.

They looked at one another, confounded.

Longarm insisted, "It's just after noon. As I understand the times to tally, Lem Redfern and Dick Lloyd left here last night no later than eight or nine. That would put them at your relay station west of here around when, no later than ten or eleven?"

The white wrangler answered, "Earlier. They rolled in around quarter to ten. It took us four minutes to change the team, but one pesky lady spent close to seven in the shithouse. We had them on their way around ten. Neither me nor Bob, here, was there. But Lem Redfern told us they forded the La Plata and drove six or seven miles, or the better part of an hour, making it ten-forty-five or so when they met up with them same road agents at about the same place as the last time!"

The breed called Bob looked up at Longarm to volunteer, "This time Lem was driving down that grade instead of walking his passenger and mules up it. I wish we *had* been there. It must have looked comical as hell when that fool in the kachina mask popped out on the trail in the moonlight, ordering Lem to stand and deliver!"

The white wrangler snickered and said, "Lem never. He snapped his old whip and tried to run over the rascal who'd gunned Tom Cartier. I reckon I'd have jumped out of the way too! Then that new hand, Dick Lloyd, blazed away with his Greener ten-gauge and blew the buck-naked bastard ass-over-teakettle with both barrels!''

Longarm wrote down ''Circa 11 P.M.'' and quietly asked, ''How come it took you over twelve hours to drive in no more than twelve miles with the news?''

The one called Bob flashed his dark eyes like a flamenco dancer and snapped, ''You try driving twelve miles in the dark with outlaws acting *loco en la cabeza* all around! It was way after midnight before we knew a thing about it, at our relay station. Lem and his shotgun messenger drove that coach a ways before they calmed down and considered what a lead they were giving the road agents by not turning back to report a second try at our line.''

''There's no telegraph line this side of Sevier Junction,'' the white boy explained. He added, ''Lem and Dick Lloyd rolled in after midnight, with their passengers on the prod with gun barrels out the windows on all sides. They told our station manager, Harry Bekins. He had us give them fresh mules and sent 'em on, overdue. We were fixing to drive in at daybreak. But at dawn old Ruby, the Ute squaw who cooks and sews for old Harry at the station, spotted something or somebody lurking out in the chaparral. So we all forted up, and waited. Then we waited some more until old Harry allowed we couldn't wait all day and told us to drive in and tell everybody what had happened. He never told us to expect no Spanish Inquisition.''

''I do not ride for His Most Catholic Majesty. I ride for President Rutherford B. Hayes and U.S. Marshal William Vail, both of whom need to know just as much about sinners in these parts,'' said Longarm in a friendly but firm voice.

Turning to a blank page, he continued, ''I need a clearer notion of your timetable. Start me east from this Sevier Junction in the Mormon Delta aboard one of your luxurious Concord coaches, old son.''

The two young wranglers stared at one another, confused. An older gent in a suit and tie intervened from the crowd to introduce himself as the Durango station manager.

He said, ''You can't expect local help who seldom ride a dozen miles of our better-than-two-hundred to tell you all that much about it.''

Longarm shrugged and said, ''Why don't you try, then? Is your timetable supposed to be a state secret?''

The station manager, who also had to sell tickets, smiled wistfully and replied, ''We try for a hundred and twenty miles a day. If you got on around dawn in Sevier Junction we'd feed you a simple but wholesome noon dinner at our scenic station on the Escalante rimrocks. Then we'd roll you faster down the Escalante River, it goes down into the ground a ways. Then the going gets a tad slower once you've forded the Colorado down in Glen Canyon and started up some more. So you'd lay over for the night at our Clay Hills home station, enjoy your second dinner at Bluff Creek, and drive along the north cliffs of the San Juan until the trail forks due east for here, with relay stops every fifteen miles or less until we get you here in time to connect with that night train to the east.''

Longarm nodded thoughtfully and asked, ''Let's say I came in aboard the same train one afternoon and wanted to ride on west by coach with you all.''

The station manager replied, ''We'd put you aboard our coach that came in around the same time. We run it west as a night coach for the same reasons the D&RGW runs their afternoon train back as their night train. Saves on rolling stock. Men and mules need to rest up after a long hard run. Wheels don't, as long as you grease 'em once in a while.''

''Then you're running the same coach both ways, constant?'' Longarm asked.

The older man shook his head and said, ''We own four. One at Sevier Junction in run-down condition, to be salvaged for spare parts as need be. We keep one better Concord as a spare and have two out on the trail at all times.''

Longarm started to ask why, but nodded and put his notebook away as he murmured, ''Right. Two days from here to yonder calls for a coach to be leaving your home station every time one starts from either end. By overlapping night and day runs you don't need to have two coaches using the same station facilities at the same time. But don't that work hell out of your station crews, no offense?''

A kid in bib overalls who seemed to work there laughed wearily. But his better-dressed boss explained, ''We have night and day shifts to roll our wheels and manage the passengers and stock. A new Concord coach sells for thirteen hundred dollars. You can hire lots of station help for less and, even if we had more coaches, the passengers and express we carry are in a hurry. How would it look if we made westbound fares getting off the afternoon train waste twenty-four whole hours here in Durango?''

Longarm soothed, ''I never told you not to run any night coaches. I was agreeing it made sense. I was only trying to consider your timetable as a road agent might.''

The mollified station manager asked what he'd figured out.

Longarm said, ''Nothing I didn't know when I came in here just now. I'd already figured the gang was operating closer to this end of your long lonely line. It gets rougher and even less civilized as you move west. So they must be attracted by an easier getaway over this way than you'd find in, say, the depths of Glen Canyon.''

The older man, who knew his stage route better, said, ''Much of that canyon country west of our Clay Hills home station has never really been surveyed, or even looked at, by white riders.''

To which Longarm replied, ''I just said that. There's heaps of country closer you could hide whole towns in.

50

White riders are always coming across Indian ghost towns betwixt here and them cliff dwellings up Hovenweep Canyon in the Utah Territory. So it's been a pleasure talking to you. But I got me some riding to do.''

Back at the county corral he found Deputy Malone, the newspaper gal, and a half dozen riders waiting on him and ready to go. Malone had picked matching bay ponies for Longarm, with the spare naturally barebacked and the other saddled with a Muller roper. The throw rope still leathered to the swells was braided hemp the color of strong tea. They'd issued him a Winchester '73, chambered for the same .44-40 rounds as his six-gun and riding in a saddle boot with its stock jutting above the low roping cantle ahead of a bedroll they'd made up clean for him, they said.

He didn't argue. He said he was sorry for holding up the parade, and they all mounted up and rode out to the west of Durango before one P.M.

They rode west along the rutted wagon trace in a column of twos, with each rider trailing his spare mount. So when Longarm found himself staring up the ass of Malone's trailing roan, with Phaedra Thorne beside him, sidesaddle, they were free to talk dirty, or at least in private, with their own spares betwixt them and the following pair of riders. So he asked their visitor from London what she knew about the blustery cuss in short chinked chaps who'd fallen in to Malone's left, as if he thought he was their leader.

She said she only knew they called him Chinks and added she'd been told the junior officer rode to the left of his superior.

Longarm said, "I ain't sure about Queen Victoria's cavalry columns. When *we* move out this way, the right-hand forward rider is called the guidon. Everyone dresses or lines up on him, leaving the leader free to just . . . lead.''

She pointed out that neither rider in front of them was carrying a guidon pennant. He decided that might mean

Malone thought he was in the lead position. It was no skin off anyone else's nose.

Whoever thought he was in charge set an uncomfortable mile-eating pace. So Longarm didn't get to talk too much to the gal on his right as they both trotted their mounts. He had the choice of standing all the way in the stirrups or letting the saddle paddle his ass. There was something to be said for the sidesaddle they'd rustled up for the English gal, at a trot. She had her left foot in the one stirrup with her right knee hooked over its padded rest, so's only one half of her shapely ass was in contact with her mount and, thanks to the lopsided but firm bracing, moving in time with the same.

She sure sat a horse pretty.

Less than a full hour out, it was Chinks, not Malone, who raised his free hand like he thought he was George Armstrong Custer and had everyone rein in, about halfway to that first stage stop on the La Plata. In the confusion that followed Longarm learned Chinks was the head wrangler for the sheriff's department. It had been him, not the deputy in command of the posse, who'd selected and saddled their riding stock for them. So Longarm forgave old Chinks for seeming to feel so uppity. He had no call to tell the boisterous cuss he was sorry, since he'd never called him anything mean, to his face.

With Chinks blustering uncalled-for orders, Longarm unsaddled the gal's dapple gray as well as his own bay gelding. She knew why both saddles sunned upside down in the grass off the wagon trace as they all enjoyed a sit-down and a smoke, with nobody commenting on those who felt the call to nature, further out in the chaparral.

After a ten-minute trail break they saddled the spare mounts they'd been leading and mounted up to trot the last six miles or less within an hour. So it was around three in the afternoon when they rode on in to the relay station on the banks of the brawling brown La Plata.

The fat man of around forty who ran the station, Harry Bekins, had nothing new to offer on the topic of road agents, but allowed his Ute serving wench, a moonfaced old gal they called Ruby, dressed up in a white apron and black Mother Hubbard, would be proud to feed them an early supper.

So they let her, as most of them sat around the long plank table out front, under a lattice ramada, comparing notes on shot-up kachina dancers and which way they might have run off with all that buckshot on board.

Bekins opined, "They never rode east. This is about the only easy ford across the La Plata for many a mile, and we were watching it. I can't speak for the many miles of nothing much to the west, though."

Kevin Malone brought up the Mesa Verde some more. Bekins allowed he just couldn't say that much about the Mesa Verde. It was a score or more miles west-sou'west and he'd never been there. He called out to old Ruby. When she came out front with a pot in one hand he asked her to tell them what she and her own folk had to say about the Mesa Verde.

Ruby didn't hesitate to say, "*Puha ka hoo!* Bad medicine! No real people have ever lived there! Never! Some say bones of *Hodukam*, those who used to eat real people, walk the canyons on those nights there is no moon. Others say *Piamuhmpitz*, the spirit owl who eats children, makes its nest on top of the mesa. If I were you I would not play *nanipka* with ghosts of Hodukam around the Mesa Verde!"

Longarm explained to the others that she was talking about extinct cannibals, or stories handed down about ancient ogres. Nobody really knew all that much about the long lost cliff dwellers.

Deputy Malone said he'd always hankered to arrest him a cannibal. Longarm suggested they start with the way closer scene of that last attempted stagecoach robbery.

Malone didn't argue. So they polished off the son-of-a-bitch stew and sourdough biscuits Ruby served with tolerable coffee and got set to ford the La Plata and scout for sign on the far side before sundown.

They'd changed their saddles back to the original and now less tired ponies. As he helped her mount up, out front, Longarm warned Phaedra the river water might come high as her stirrup, thanks to that recent rain. He told her to hang on to her saddle's low pommel if she and her mount lost their footing. She drily remarked she'd been riding since childhood. It would have been rude to ask her where, or on what, so he never did, and they were soon on their way down the clay bank of the muddy La Plata, with her behind Malone and Chinks but ahead of Longarm as they led their spare ponies single file.

Phaedra was likely right about her own riding skills. It wasn't her who made the first wrong move. The jaded pony she was leading balked at the sudden slippery incline. Phaedra gave its lead line a gentle yank. The spooked pony responded in spades, lurching forward to bump the rump of Phaedra's mount and throw it off balance with its forehooves in the swirling water and its hind end high in the air.

So the next thing anyone knew, Phaedra's infernal roan was trying to imitate a duck, head down in the brawling brown river, with Phaedra grabbing for and missing her pommel entire!

Then she went all the way under to come up a few yards downstream, thrashing and carrying on as if she were drowning. Which, come to study on it, she seemed to be getting at, as the swift current swept her not too merrily down the stream.

Chapter 7

Longarm let go of his spare mount and shook out a couple of coils of throw rope as he galloped south along the bank after the thrashing visitor from London. A couple of other riders were right behind him and none of them were having much luck. For while the current carried Phaedra no more than eight or ten miles an hour, it carried her direct and you couldn't ride through trees and boulders along the steep left bank of the infernal La Plata!

There had to be a better way. He shucked his hat, coat, and gun rig, even as he was reining in. Then he shed his vest and took a running jump into the river as he heard someone yelling, "Have you gone out of your fool head, Longarm? She's a good furlong down the river ahead of you and nobody swims fast as a pony can run!"

This was the simple truth, Longarm knew, as he proceeded to swim after the distant bobbing head of the now hatless Phaedra Thorne. Up above them, on dry land, would-be rescuers were rapidly left behind as the swift current whipped them around a rocky bend.

But there was method in Longarm's apparent madness,

provided the frightened girl downstream could only keep her head above water a spell. For, as he'd already noticed, Phaedra was treading water, with the current doing all the work of carrying her lickety-split in the general direction of the distant Sea of Cortez by way of the Grand Canyon. He, on the other hand, was enjoying the same free ride down the La Plata, while *swimming* in the same current.

He hadn't taken time to shuck his boots before jumping in after Phaedra. But they didn't drown him when they filled up because the rampaging water wasn't deep enough. He was able to kick his way along the rocky bottom as the rest of him sort of swam downstream. For the first million years he didn't seem to be gaining on the floundering brunette. But Phaedra was touching bottom now and again to *resist* the current. So Longarm slowly closed the distance between them until he caught up, somewhere down the damned river, and told her to hang on to him while he tried to swim them at an angle.

She sputtered, "I thought I was done for! What happened to my poor horse?"

He sputtered back, "Can't say for certain. But you seemed to be swirling downstream on your own. So I reckon it made its way to one bank or the other. It had four longer legs to work with. Let's just worry about us for now. I see some willow branches dangling to the water on the convex bank of the bend coming up. Let your feet float so's you don't shove us any way I ain't trying to!"

She let herself go limp below the surface, clinging wetly to his neck and shoulders as he thrashed harder. At first she didn't think they were going to make it. Then she thought there was an outside chance and marveled, "My stars and garters, you're so *strong*!"

Longarm didn't answer. As the muddy water carried them under the dangling willow branches, he kicked hard against the bottom and managed to grab hold and hang on while the current swung them on to shallower slack water.

She almost lost her grip on his wet shirt as he climbed higher, hanging on to slippery willow whips. He let go with one hand to grab her around her tiny waist and discovered without a lick of dismay that she wasn't wearing a corset under her soggy riding habit after all. But this seemed a dumb time to feel a gal up. So he got them both out of the river, somewhere along the west bank, and then he helped her through the tangle of willows to see if they could figure out where else they might be.

There was maybe three or four yards of grass and brush-covered marl betwixt the undercut riverbank and a vertical sandstone cliff the color and texture of old brown paper bags. It was tough to see up or downstream worth mention, thanks to the way the damned stream curved. The opposite bank was as overgrown near the water and as hemmed in by canyon wall just beyond. He told Phaedra, "We seem to have fetched up in a narrow gut. There were some riders chasing after us, way back when. They might be able to work their way this far down. If they can I'll ask 'em to go back up to the ford, cross over, and lead our ponies down this bank to us."

She glanced up at the sky and said, "I hope they hurry. It will be getting dark in just a few more hours. What if they've given us both up for swept away and drowned? I know that's what I was expecting when you suddenly showed up, you loverly man!"

Longarm said, "Aw, mush, let's see how far upstream we can make it on our own. Your point about them giving us up for lost is well taken, and I ain't sure I'd want to ride a pony south along this brushy narrow ledge. Hang on to my shirttails. They'll dry faster if I let 'em hang out, and it's too tricky along this cliff to stroll hand in hand."

She unbuttoned her bodice and let the hem of her white blouse hang outside her soggy, black broadcloth skirt before she took hold of his shirttails as directed and they started squishing back upstream.

It wasn't easy. Their soaked-through boots would have made it tough enough. The narrow strip of footing at the base of the cliff was soft sod where it wasn't overgrown with everything brushy from willow to catclaw and soapweed, as the shorter but no duller version of yucca was called this far north of the border.

They passed a cleft in the cliff and Phaedra asked if he could hear that ghostly humming too. Forging on, he explained, "The canyon wall is sucking cooler air off the water after a long dry day under the summer sun. Up top, where the rimrocks have baked hot enough to fry eggs, such air as there is keeps rising, fast. These smaller erosion channels are getting sucked like soda straws from their tops. So they suck cooler air sideways to make up for it."

She allowed she understood, but wondered if the mysterious moaning might not account for some of the stories about those haunted cliff dwellings off to the west.

He said, "Wait 'til you meet up with your first mummified cliff dweller. I was building a night fire under an overhang one dark and windy night when I suddenly noticed this dead lady in a turkey feather robe grinning down at me from a higher niche. Nobody has to make any noises at such times. But of course these tricky canyon breezes and the flutterings of bats and pack rats might inspire even more ghost stories. After that, Indians are more uneasy about dead folk than we are."

She said very few of her own kith and kin seemed comfortable around mummified cadavers or things that went bump in the night.

He said, "Indians find Mister Death even more dismaying, only most nations describe Death as an ugly old woman. When one of us cashes in, the friends and relations gather around for the reading of the will. A dead Indian gets to keep everything he owned. I've seen mounds where they buried a chief, sitting up, on his best pony. Nobody wants the toys or treasures of a dead Indian, unless he's a white man collecting for a museum, or his own curio cabinet. So there's still heaps of old-time pottery, prayer sticks, and such, tucked away from here to the Hovenweep ruins, along with the original owners.''

He shoved through a tangle of willow to stop and move back as he muttered, "End of the line. Cliff drops clear to the water just up ahead. There has to be a better way."

She gasped, "We have to make our way back before sunset, Custis!"

He replied, "I just said that. Let's try crawling into the pumpkin. It'll be easier for you to turn around and take the lead than for me to scramble around you on this crumblesome ledge."

She let go his shirt and started edging back the way they'd come, even as she asked him what pumpkin they were talking about.

Longarm patted the wall of sandstone to his right as he explained, "This rock formation runs clear down into Navaho Country, turning more orange as it does so. The Navaho call it Pumpkin Rock."

They got back to the cleft. He said, "It's riddled like Swiss cheese by time and rainwater. So you can sort of crawl through it in some parts. The Navaho who showed me how called it crawling into the pumpkin. Let's see where we come out if we crawl in here."

She didn't seem to cotton to the notion. He took the lead and told her, "It's safe enough as long as it ain't raining. Like I said, rainwater did all this, and I'd say we've had enough running water for one day."

She sighed and replied, "I shan't argue with that! I'm absobloodylutely *freezing* in these wet clothes! It's funny, I thought this habit was too warm for the afternoon sun before I fell in that ice water like a chump!"

He said, "Wasn't your fault, entire. As to how icy you may feel, this draft following us along this cleft ain't really that cold. We're over a mile above sea level, even down here in this crack. So the air's more thin and dry than cold. You run out of breath with less effort and your wet duds feel colder than they ought to for the same reasons water boils sooner and takes longer to cook a three-minute egg at this altitude. Water evaporates faster, at lower temperature, in thinner air.''

She said she'd just noticed that as she followed him upward as well as inward through the smoothly sculpted natural passageway. Such light as there was sliced down through the wavy narrow slit far above them. Apart from the narrowness of their natural skylight, the sky up yonder was becoming ominously lavender.

When she commented on that, Longarm told her, ''I noticed. But we seem to be climbing, to the southwest, I fear. We ought to make the top before it's really dark. If this low mesa was broad enough for us to get lost on top of, it would be more famous.''

As they rounded a serpentine bend Longarm spotted a scattered tangle of bones ahead and warned her calmly, ''The skeleton you're about to meet up with ain't human. A coyote, or mayhaps a dog, was likely flash flooded down here a spell back.''

He stepped over the scattered bones and didn't look back as he heard Phaedra exclaim, ''Oh, the poor thing! I thought you said dead bodies mummified up in these canyons, Custis.''

He said, ''This ain't a canyon, it's a drainage cleft, and I never said *all* dead bodies dry out before they can spoil. It's all in how you *store* meat here in this pumpkin rock. Leave dead folk or a bag of spuds where water can get at 'em and they'll spoil about as soon as you might expect. But tuck 'em into a niche where the rain never falls and no water ever runs and they'll keep for hundreds of years. This thin air sucks moisture out of animal, vegetable, or mineral like a thirsty blotter.''

She asked, ''Even in damp weather?''

He thought, shrugged, and decided, "Nobody's ever found a *perfectly* preserved cliff dweller. But they never pick up enough moisture that way to decay worth mention. Were you planning on opening a funeral parlor out this way, Miss Phaedra?"

She laughed and declared she was in the market for a Turkish bathhouse at the moment. He agreed the thought of changing from wet tweed pants to fluffy white towel after a nice warm steam bath made him wish he had one of those magic lamps to rub. Then he changed the subject. It was pesky to take long strides with a hard-on, and there was hardly any way a man could picture taking a steam bath with Phaedra Thorne without getting a hard-on.

The channel they were exploring got narrower and steeper as they followed it ever onward and upward. When they came to a fork, Longarm chose the narrower of the two branches. Phaedra asked him why. So he explained, "Rainwater carves deeper and wider as it flows. The water as carved this branch couldn't have run as far."

He proved himself right a hundred yards on, when they found their heads almost level with the lower walls to either side. Longarm felt no call to follow the winding erosion channel farther than they needed to. So he reached up, grabbed some rimrock, and hauled himself up atop a flat stoney expanse dotted with dwarfish juniper and pinyon trees.

He rolled over on his gut and extended a hand down to Phaedra. As he hauled her out of the pumpkin she glanced westward to exclaim, "Oh, what a glorious sunset, and where in the bloody hell *are* we?"

He rose and helped her to her feet, saying, "Watch your step. The light's getting tricky and we don't want to go down any other sewers. We seem to be atop a modest mesa, somewhere downstream from the La Plata relay station. That has to be to our north. So I vote we head that way, for openers."

He got no argument from the visitor from London, who tagged after him through the trees, saying, "I see what you mean about the drying effects of this thin air. But my socks and unmentionables are still wet and terribly uncomfortable!"

Without looking back, he declared, "It's best to let wet boots dry with your feet in 'em, keeping the leather working, for reasons any old trail hand could verify. As for your unmentionables, feel free to hunker down behind any handy tree and just peel 'em off. I'll neither peek nor tell a soul what you might or might not have on under such a modest riding habit."

She laughed like a mean little kid and told him he was just awful. He'd just told her he wouldn't peek. So he never turned around when she dropped back a ways. She didn't say, when she caught up with him again, what she'd done with her damp underdrawers. But he didn't hear her complaining about them anymore. So he figured she'd done something sensible.

Then he froze between two fortunately stout junipers and hung on to either side as he regarded the gut-wrenching drop just ahead and warned Phaedra, "Don't come no closer! We just run out of rimrock and we have to find another way down."

She peered north under his braced right arm and sobbed, "Oh, I can *see* that relay station up the river! That *is* where someone just lit a lamp behind an open doorway, isn't it?"

Longarm stared morosely at the low sprawl of 'dobes and corrals in the distant gathering dusk and decided, "That dust rising rosy off to the east would be their coach from the Mormon Delta, right on time tonight. I wonder where Malone and the others are right now."

She sighed and said, "I wish they were looking for us, the sods! Do you think they could be, or do you think they've given us up for dead, Custis?"

He moved them both back from the treacherous rim as

the distant lamplight winked out. He said, "They've shut the door against the night chill, over yonder. I can't tell you where Malone and the others might be right now. But if I was him, I'd figure anyone being swept around the bend like so would have either drowned or made his or her way back by this time. I reckon I'd send word back to Durango, then ride on, leaving Harry Bekins and his station crew to comfort anyone who came limping in this late."

She sighed and asked, "Why don't we start limping, then?"

He shook his bare head and told her, "You don't limp worth mention after falling down a cliff. If I had a match or a gun to my name right now, I'd try to signal to 'em from up here. But I don't. So I can't."

She sighed and said, "So near and yet so far! Are you trying to tell me we're stuck up here for the night, Custis?"

To which he could only reply, "I ain't *trying*. I'm telling you it just wouldn't be safe, or even sane, to try crawling down off this island in the sky in the dark!"

She stared soberly west at the crimson sky, as the first stars were winking on above them, to ask where they'd ever manage to sup or sleep up here in the starry sky.

He led her back through the trees to get them both out of the night winds they could expect as he told her, soothingly, "We just et some grub before we wound up in the river. We won't starve to death before morning. A night without sleep won't kill us neither. But I doubt that'll happen. You can sleep most anywhere if you have nothing better to do, and Lord knows there ain't no opera house up here."

Chapter 8

Longarm's pocketknife had gone down the river with him in his pants. He was glad it had as he cut bough after pinyon bough a safe dozen yards back from the rim. It wasn't easy. So it helped a man warm up a mite in just his shirtsleeves as the evening breezes got to swirling through the scrubby trees all around.

Phaedra could only pace back and forth. She couldn't see what he was doing well enough to say he was doing anything wrong. Their duds were now dried out to just chilly in the thirsty thin atmosphere of the Four Corners country. So she'd tucked her blouse back in her skirt and buttoned the bodice of her riding habit. She said it only helped a little and plaintively asked if it was true that pinyon pine nuts were good to eat.

Cutting away another forked branch endowed with long soft needles, Longarm grumbled, "They would be if the squirrels, canyon jays, and cross beak birds had left us any. The Indians keep careful watch and knock the cones down just as they're getting set to open. The critters enjoy them just as much. But at least we've plenty of pine needles to bed down on whilst we listen to our stomachs growl and wait for the dawn to enlighten our way down to breakfast. I sure hope we find our ponies and possibles up at that relay station as well.''

She said, ''Oh, Lord, what if I've lost all those sketches I drew for this story? I had my sketch pad in its oilcloth portfolio inside a saddlebag, but my horse could have floated off with everything, for all I know!''

Longarm cut a last branch and dropped it atop the others in the dark, soothing, ''I'd have noticed if either of our ponies bobbed off after you, Miss Phaedra. How bad might it hurt your sketches if they got sort of wet despite your careful wrapping?''

She said, ''Well, art paper is made to dry wrinkle free after you lay on a good wash. Neither my penciled nor India-inked lines ought to bleed, and I can probably restore any watercolors that I have, once I get my perishing work *back*! Are you sure we'll find them at that relay station, Custis?''

To which he could only reply, ''Nope. But that's where they ought to be, unless they're with Deputy Malone and his riders. Others were watching as we both parted company with our ponies and possibles and, even if they hadn't been, riderless mounts tend to head for the nearest fodder and water, which would be up yonder at that relay station. Let's not worry about who might be hanging on to our stuff for us. Somebody has to be and there's hardly any Quill Indians left in these parts at the moment. Why don't we set ourselves down on this feather bed I've just fashioned. I piled the pine boughs in the lee of this rabbit bush with the prevailing night winds in mind.''

She sat down beside him, bounced experimentally, and declared the experiment a success. Then she reached behind them to finger a sprig of rabbit bush and ask why they called it rabbit bush. Newspaper folk were like that.

When he explained you found jackrabbits around the

stuff because it gave good cover a rabbit could nibble, Phaedra broke off a twig, chewed it thoughtfully, and decided the bloody rabbits could speak for themselves.

She snuggled closer to add, "I'm bleeding *cold* as well. I'm sure we'd both be warmer if we lay flat together, snuggled up a bit more. But I have to warn you, I've a bloke back home in Blighty."

Longarm put one arm around her shoulder and reclined the two of them below the swaying tips of the rabbit bush branches as he calmly replied, "That's jake with me. I have a blokess or so back in Denver."

She laughed and said, "That's what I've heard about you. One of the chambermaids at our hotel in Durango tells me you're quite Jack the Lad with the ladies."

Longarm thought, frowned up at the stars, and firmly decided that he'd never left either of the two drabs back at that hotel in position to comment on his private life.

When he said as much, Phaedra confided, "One of them told me you and a Durango waitress were the talk of the town."

Longarm sighed and muttered, "Oh, Lord, there seem to be three rival means of rapid communication these days. Telegraph, telephone, and tell-a-woman! For the record, I lost any interest I'd ever had in the lady in question when yet another Durango gal told me there was a serious rival to consider."

Phaedra said, "I'm still freezing. Have you considered that big Swede's true love could have been the one who pegged a shot at you the other day in Durango?"

Longarm hugged her a tad tighter as he replied, "I have and he couldn't. He was coming west aboard the D&RGW when somebody who just couldn't have been him pegged a shot at somebody gathered near that taproom window with us. How do you know it wasn't your bloke from London, sore at you for acting so friendly to such a crude cuss?"

She softly replied, "I hadn't made up my mind about you, yet. I don't know how *crude* you might be, Custis. But I must say you're a little *slow*."

So he rolled half atop her to kiss her and she kissed him back, in the French manner. But then, as he let his free hand wander inside her half-buttoned bodice, she pulled her lips from his to protest, "Wait! We have to talk about my bloke in Blighty!"

Longarm grumbled, "How come? I ain't trying to get warm with him, or even a blokess back in Denver. No offense, Miss Phaedra, but you were the one who complained about my acting shy. I was aiming to be polite. I ain't one for tomfool gallantries at times like this. I leave it to the lady to set the pace and choose the tune. You and that chambermaid would be surprised how many times I've escorted a lady to and from a Sunday-Go-to-Meeting-on-the-Green without ripping her bodice like a beast or even kissing her on the cheek. But I ain't no sissy neither. So do you want me to make love to you or not? We both know you're good-looking. But there ain't no gal good-looking enough to make me jump through hoops like her poodle dog!"

She gasped, "Blimey, I was only trying to set some ground rules, not start a perishing war! I only meant to warn you not to take anything a girl away from home might do too . . . serious."

He thought, then asked, "Oh, are you trying to say it won't mean we're engaged or even courting serious if we just swap some spit up here, in private, to keep warm?"

She laughed sort of wild and declared, "I couldn't have put it more romantically. Swap some spit with me, you adorable ninny!"

So they did and this time when he felt for her firm little breast she not only let him but asked why he was acting slow again. So he ran his hand down, hauled her broadcloth skirt up, and discovered to their mutual delight that he'd been right about her shucking those damp underdrawers.

Thanks to the thin dry air her considerable pubic thatch was dry and, thanks to their dunking in the river, all their naked flesh was clean and smelling swell as he undressed them both. It was only after he'd rolled atop to enter her warm depths with his chilled erection that he felt safe to ask her why she hadn't mentioned that revolver she'd been packing all this time in one pocket of her habit.

Hugging him tighter with both her arms and shapely legs, her damp boots still on, Phaedra calmly asked why he hadn't used it to signal for help before taking advantage of such a poor frigid lass.

He laughed, kissed her dirty, and pounded her harder as he growled, "If it's one thing you ain't, it's frigid, no offense. But that's jake with this child. For you may have noticed I ain't cold-natured neither. As for trying to attract attention in the dark with your bitty pearl-handled pissoliver, I wanted to screw you more than I wanted to get down off this mesa. Am I forgiven?"

She moaned, "I'll forgive you if you do it to me faster, more than once! I don't feel at all cold or hungry now! Why can't we just stay up here and screw all night?"

He started to say something dumb. Then he finished coming in her, rolled her over on her naked belly and breasts, and entered her some more from behind, saying, "Safer climbing down by daylight, with or without help, and ain't nobody tracking nobody now that it's too dark to try."

She arched her spine and thrust her shapely little derriere skyward, sobbing, "Oh, that feels so big and loverly, darling. If I call you darling, out here under the stars, do you think you can remember I don't really love you, Custis?"

He got a better grip on her hipbones and thrust in and out with more vigor as he replied, "That sounds fair to me. But I have to say I really *like* pretty ladies who screw so fine without asking a man to make false promises!"

She hissed, "Faster! Faster and promise me the moon, you rascal! I said I didn't want us to fall in love. I never said not to love and be loved in return as you make me come, again and again, until I beg you to stop and you just ravage me some more!"

He figured she'd been reading some of those romantic novels with plain brown wrappers. So he rolled her on her back some more to fork an elbow under either of her dainty knees and pay her no mind when she protested she was no blinking bloody wishbone.

She yelled aloud, "Godstrikeabloodylight! You're touching bottom with every fucking stroke and I can't tell if I'm having an orgasm or suffering a rupture, but I love it and I'll never forgive you if you stop!"

But of course he had to, after they'd both come. Then she was on top, balanced on her hunkered heels, Indian style, as she literally jerked him hard again with her whole beautiful bouncing body.

They finished the old-fashioned way, for a novel change, and then they snuggled naked under her ample broadcloth skirt with his shirt and her blouse stuffed with pine needles for pillows.

They caught some fitful sleep, interspersed by more love-making. Then it was dawn and they were both starving, but the morning light inspired a spell of mighty friendly sunbathing.

Then they just had to get dressed and go looking for something to eat. The same bright light that made Phaedra's bitty bare rump so appealing made it easy for Longarm to find the headwater erosion of another twisted channel leading downward to the north. Once they followed it to lower ground, it took less than half an hour to leg it back upstream to the wagon trace and ford.

A thoughtful wrangler at the relay station spotted them a good ways off and ran a buckboard into the now shallower La Plata so the three of them could cross back dry-shod.

Everybody else was waiting for them on the far bank. The jovial Harry Bekins said they'd been given up for lost when they'd failed to return by sundown.

The beefy station manager explained, "Nobody stays afloat all that far in that river when it's running high water. It ain't that it's so deep. It's so *rocky*. Now and again a body fetches up on a sandbar, down as far as the bigger San Juan. Most of them look more beat to death than drownded. Deputy Malone sent word to town about the two of you. But we got your riding stock out back, and you'll find your saddles and possibles in our tack room."

Phaedra was anxious to see how her artwork had made out. Longarm had been feeling naked without his hat and .44-40, even when he wasn't on top of Phaedra. So they followed Bekins around to the tack room of their stable whilst old Ruby rustled up some breakfast for them.

Phaedra found her sketchbook had gotten wet when her saddlebags flooded, then dried out again, wrinkled. This hadn't hurt her sketches all that much. For as she'd foreseen, most of her pencil and pen work was waterproof. She asked Harry Bekins if she could have a bucket of water. He sent one of his wranglers out to the pump. Longarm had put his vest, guns, coat, and hat back on by the time the artistic little thing was slopping pump water all over the drawings she'd been so worried about.

As they all watched, bemused, the newspaper illustrator spread each soggy sheet of drawing paper flat on a loose plank they'd found for her as well. When Bekins asked how come, Phaedra explained the wet paper, stretched drumhead tight and flat as ever, would soon dry flat in the thin thirsty air.

Longarm stared thoughtfully down at her lined up illustrations. He knew most of the faces she'd sketched. She'd sketched them good. So he figured she had that kachina mask and body tattoos as close. He took her pencil's word on those Mormons and the late Tom Cartier the cuss in the kachina mask had gunned.

Then old Ruby bawled out the back that breakfast was being served. So they went around to her outdoor table and got to work on her bacon and sourdough biscuits with coffee strong enough to strip paint.

Harry Bekins allowed he'd have a second breakfast to be polite. It was small wonder Harry and old Ruby were so stout. Whilst the three of them ate, Longarm got more details out of the jovial fat man.

The coach from the Mormon Delta had rolled in the evening before, not long after Phaedra had rolled into the river, with less to worry about. The other Jehu, Lem Redfern being over in the Clay Hills home station by now, had reported no signs of menace anywhere along his long day on the trail.

Longarm almost let that go. Then he asked, "Don't you mean a *two*-day run, Mr. Bekins? I thought it was over two hundred miles from Durango to Sevier Junction in the Utah Territory."

Bekins washed down a heroic mouthful, suppressed a belch, and replied, "It's two hundred miles and change. Our coaches are made of ashwood, hickory, and iron. Our mules and men ain't. We trot our teams fifteen miles a day and expect a hard day on and a hard day off from a crew. So the Jehu and shotgun messenger make a twelve-hour run and lay over at either end. Lem and that new boy, Dick Lloyd, will be rolling in here this evening after laying over at the midway home station, if you want to talk to them some more."

Longarm turned to Phaedra, who shrugged and said she hadn't been paying much attention after a dreadful night on a lumpy mattress at that awful overnight stop. She said, "We'd spent a long weary day on the trail, a lot of it careening down canyons, but, now that you've mentioned it,

I *do* think we started out with another crew. I wasn't paying much attention as they woke us up at daybreak, halfway here."

Longarm had just decided it hardly mattered who might be driving when a coach got robbed when one of the wranglers came over to tell them, "Rider coming in from the west. Moving right along!"

So they all got up and moved closer to the river for a better view. You could see the dust before you could make out a lone rider on a paint pony. As he got closer they agreed it was one of the boys from Durango who'd been riding with Deputy Malone and the rest of his posse.

He spurred his paint across the foaming brown ford, reined in with a startled look when he spied Longarm and the girl, and called out, "We thought you two was dead!"

Longarm smiled up at him to reply, "So did we. Where might you be headed in such a hurry, old son?"

The posse rider on the paint replied, "Into town to get more help. It wasn't easy, but we finally cut their trail, and there's more than a dozen of the sons of . . . Sorry, ladies. The essence of Malone's message is that he figures he's outnumbered better than two to one, and I think it was U.S. Grant who said the attacking force ought to be the bigger one. I know it was George Armstrong Custer who *proved* it."

Chapter 9

Longarm could offer a dozen reasons why Phaedra should have gone back to Durango with the message rider. Phaedra could only come up with one good reason to tag along with Longarm.

She wanted to.

So whilst he roped their four ponies and saddled two, the stubborn newspaper gal thumbtacked her damp drawings to that board and got old Harry Bekins to swear he'd guard them for her with his life.

Longarm asked old Ruby if she'd sell him some of her sourdough mix and a sack of flour to take along. She looked insulted and told him nobody of her nation would take money from *Saltu ka Saltu*, adopted *tua* of Chief Ouray.

Phaedra had been listening. But she waited until they'd shook hands all around, mounted up, and forded the La Plata with good wishes shouted after them before she asked what Ruby had been talking about.

Longarm shrugged and told her, "All this country you see around us used to belong to her Ute Nation. Chief Ouray and most of 'em tried to get along with us. Ouray loaned Kit Carson some fine Ute scouts when the Navaho last rose up. They all fought and some died for these United States of A. So some of us tried to keep that in mind when other Ute acted up under Colorow and Nicaagat, over by the White River Agency. We lost, of course, just as the disgruntled Ute who took on the combined Bureau of Indian Affairs and the U.S. Cavalry should have known they would. They handed the Colorado Powers-That-Be a swell excuse to evict their whole nation from the west slope. Some of us who remembered the many earlier favors balanced them against three or four rapes and less than a hundred killings, and in the end the totally innocent Ute bands of Southern Colorado were granted a fraction of their old lands for a reservation. I, for one, still think they got robbed. But I reckon some of them can read, and Chief Ouray declared me his sort of adopted child. Poor old Ouray was suffering the dropsy and not long for this old world, the last I heard tell. But ain't one Ute pegged a shot my way in recent memory.''

She asked what that title Ruby had bestowed on him might mean.

He pointed at the trail ahead with his chin as he replied, ''Just some fool mumbling. I don't talk Ute, or Ho, as they say it. Ute is a Navaho word. Just like Navaho derives from what their Pueblo enemies called *them*.''

He didn't want to explain how *Saltu ka Saltu* meant ''the stranger who is not a stranger'' because he knew she'd print that in her hometown newspaper and he felt silly enough about the *Rocky Mountain News* and that guff about the Lakota calling him *Wasichu Wastey* or Good White Man. Newspaper reporters tended to make mountains out of such molehills.

They rode on for an hour, reined in so he could swap saddles and kiss her a couple of times, then rode on despite her suggestion they take another sunbath off the trail a piece.

They rode just under another hour to the slot betwixt some lower rimrock where Phaedra said her coach had been robbed. Longarm felt no call to dismount and scout for sign. There was more sign than a scout could shake a stick at. For the well-traveled wagon trace had been well traveled since that last rain.

Pointing down at any number of hoof marks aimed either way up and down the sloping trail ahead, Longarm said, "If Malone and the others found any sign to follow, they never found it here. I'll scout the left side and you watch the right as we ride on. We're looking for at least seventeen pony trails to lead on out across the unmarked surface away from this beaten track. Malone just sent word of a dozen and he's still got four riders with him."

Phaedra allowed a professional sketch artist with a fair set of specs might manage such a chore. But she'd lost her thick glasses to the muddy waters of the La Plata and couldn't see *clearly* beyond her flaming nose now.

He sighed and allowed he could likely keep an eye out for easy sign to either side. He said, "I doubt Malone and the boys with *him* would be trying to hide their tracks, and he sent word he'd tallied the ones he was trailing as way more."

But as they rode on, trotting, walking, or resting their mounts as the morning wore on, they just didn't come across any tracks of anything more mysterious than a coyote crossing the road. A few furlongs of fork-toed tracks hinted at a roadrunner keeping company with some mystery rider who hadn't left the wagon trace. Longarm knew better than to waste time on a few detours into the chaparral by a single traveler taking a piss. He figured they were half a dozen miles west of the La Plata ford when he called a halt atop the highest rise for a ways and stood taller in his stirrups, staring all about with a puzzled frown.

Phaedra slid gracefully from her sidesaddle, delicately observing she had to take a squat. Some gals felt free to talk frankly to a man after he'd screwed them dog style. But before she strode off into the chaparral she asked him what he was staring at so hard, off to their west.

Longarm settled back in his borrowed roper and said, "Not a blamed thing, and we're close to the county line too."

She said to explain that to her when she got back and skipped off through the high chaparral to suddenly vanish as Longarm dismounted as well. He watered some catclaw closer to the trail, not caring if it hurt or helped the pestiferous sticker bush, and lit a cheroot before he commenced to change saddles again. All four ponies were wearing bits and bridles to save time at times like these and make the spares easier to manage along the way.

Phaedra rejoined him, saying, "Custis, I just found the yummiest patch of springy sod. It smells like vanilla ice cream!"

He nodded and said, "Love grass. You find more of it growing out here where nobody's grazing much stock. Cows and horses like it more than we do. That's how come they call it love grass."

She said, "Oh, I thought maybe they called it that because it's so tempting to lovers who haven't made love all day!"

He started to say it wasn't for Gawd's sake high noon yet. But it was tempting fate and frigidity to tell any woman she was acting horny on you. So he said, "Let's study on that whilst we grub both our ponies and ourselves. I'll be switched with snakes if I can see where Malone and them others went. We'll take our noon break, ride on as far as the next stagecoach relay by the Rio Manco, and turn back if nobody can tell us where they went."

She kept questioning him as he broke out four oilcloth feed bags, filled them with canteen water and cracked corn, and slipped them over the stock's eager muzzles before he led them over to a patch of creosote and tethered them there

76

with the saddles upside down in the blazing sun and gentle noon breezes.

Phaedra led him over to that patch of love grass she'd discovered more by smell than myopic eyesight. A nine-by-twelve oriental rug could have fit inside the oblong oval of springy, sweet-scented and sun-cured grass. As Phaedra began to strip he looked around to make sure there was nobody watching within miles. There was something to be said for being nearsighted at times like these. Phaedra likely felt bathed in soft romantic candle-glow as she stripped down to her boots with the overhead sun illuminating every hair and imperfection of her nearly hairless and almost perfect little body. She spread her duds across the grass to dry, then lay down to spread her legs wide, smiling up at him from both ends as he shucked his own impediments and dropped down to his knees to just fall forward into her welcoming arms and thighs.

He'd forgotten how swell love grass smelled, and even how wondrous it felt to slide his old organ grinder into her moist she-male flesh, or any moist she-male flesh. For that was one of the nicest things a man or a woman kept finding out. Every time felt marvelous and new. Making love with anyone who wasn't absolutely disgusting was the one pleasure that never seemed to grow tedious.

He idly wondered why as he posted in her love-saddle with a palm hooked under either frisky buttock to help her bounce in time with him. When you thought about it, they weren't doing anything they'd never done before, a heap, with other folk as well, to hear her tell. The parts of his brain that added up his expense accounts and figured the fair prices for fresh tobacco and ammunition told him, even as he was fixing to come in her, that they were just ships passing in the night, with no future worth mention together say a week or so down the trail to nowheres. But as Phaedra kissed him, and huskily groaned that she loved him and that she'd always love him, he was able to tell her he felt the same way without crossing his fingers.

Then he told her to uncross her ankles and let go his rump, right that instant, because he heard somebody else coming, on horseback!

Longarm had good ears, and that other rider was loping his mount on a sun-baked wagon trace. For he was still a few furlongs away, on his way east, when Longarm broke cover, fully dressed and holding his borrowed Winchester '73 polite as he blocked the trail.

The stranger reined in his buckskin barb to call out, "I ain't got but six dollars to my name, and you don't have to gun me if you want it *that* bad, Mr. Winchester."

Longarm smiled reassuringly and called back, "Name's Custis Long and I'm the law, not a road agent. We're looking for a posse out of Durango. You ain't seen 'em, have you, Mister . . . ?"

"Dumont, Mike Dumont out of Iowa by way of Leadville," the older and more ragged stranger replied. He started to ask who Longarm meant by "we." Then Phaedra came out on the trail, her bodice buttoned and face innocent as a schoolmarm's. So Dumont ticked his battered gray hat brim to her as he asked Longarm if they might be talking about five riders, one of them wearing chinked chaps.

When Longarm said they were, the older man made a sweeping gesture to the west and replied, "Seen 'em a ways back, closer to that Rio Manco. Don't know as they saw me. I doubt it. I ducked. I didn't know until just now they was a posse. I've heard tell there's a band of road agents out this way!"

Longarm smiled thinly up at the brim-shaded face he just couldn't place as he answered, "So they say. Where might you have heard about such recent events?"

The rider who described himself as Mike Dumont pointed back over his shoulder with a free thumb to easily reply, "Caitlin O'Flynn at the relay station on the Rio Manco. I just asked them there about a job. Like I said, I've been working up Leadville way, heard they were paying better down here in the Four Corners country, but must have heard wrong. I've hunted high and low for work in Durango, but . . ."

"That's likely where I've seen your face before," Longarm cut in. "You say you saw them five other riders betwixt here and the relay station ahead?"

Dumont shook his head and pointed off to the southwest to reply, "They was riding through the chaparral, half a mile off, when I spied them first. I told you why I ducked them. I'd have ducked you, had I seen you first. I can't tell you who they might have been chasing. I was likely jawing with good old Caitlin O'Flynn, at the usual ford, when and if anyone forded the Rio Manco further downstream."

Longarm stared soberly at what seemed a flat far horizon. He knew better. He asked, "Are you saying Malone and his boys were chasing a dozen others toward that Mesa Verde, over yonder?"

The mounted man shrugged and answered easily, "I ain't saying anybody is doing anything. I didn't know until you told me just now who the five riders I saw might have been. I never saw anyone out ahead of 'em. So how am I to tell you where everyone was going?"

Longarm thought long and silently until Dumont asked, "Do you want me to ride back to that relay station so's they can vouch for me as an out-of-work hostler?"

Longarm said, "Ain't sure we're headed that way. You say you handle horseflesh for a living? No offense, but you've lathered that barb considerable."

Dumont patted his mount's buckskin neck and replied, "I've only been loping him since I spotted them other riders I took for road agents. I reckon me and old Buck can *walk* the rest of the way back to Durango, seeing any owlhoot riders in these parts seem to be off to the Mesa Verde.''

Longarm asked if Dumont needed any water or cracked corn. When the apparent saddle tramp said he and old Buck had plenty, Longarm stepped aside and Dumont rode on with a last polite tick of his hat brim to Phaedra as he passed her.

Longarm watched the ragged stranger and his pony recede in the distance a spell before he decided, aloud, ''It only works one way if he was telling the truth. I failed to read the signs right back at the scene of the robbery and double killing.''

She demured, ''I thought you said there were no hoof or footprints, Custis.''

He answered, ''I just said that. I only scouted along both sides of the wagon trace. I'd have seen tracks in the softer soil off the packed-down and sun-baked right-of-way, unless they led off across that rimrock to either side of the cut. Malone must have taken more time there. A better tracker than me must have found something up on the flat rock I was too lazy to dismount and crawl around on. Malone and his boys led their ponies on foot up the steep sandstone slopes and off across that flat rocky ridge until they could read the signs better. Malone wouldn't have sent that rider back to report at least a dozen outlaws if he hadn't come across the hoofprints of at least a dozen riders.''

Phaedra sighed and asked, ''Are we going to ride all the way back to that horrid slope where they murdered our armed guard and another passenger?''

Longarm shook his head and pointed toward their barely visible ponies off in the chaparral, saying, ''Not hardly. We're going to have a time catching up as it is. I'll saddle up and we'll beeline west-southwest to see if we can cut the trails of Malone and the bunch he seems to be chasing.''

As she followed him through the chaparral, he glanced thoughtfully at the now really distant Mike Dumont to tell her, "I should have insisted you ride back to Durango with that other rider we knew a mite better. He may or may not bring back more lawmen, seeing he'd know better where he parted company with Malone and the others. In the meanwhile I could be escorting a lady to a gunfight and I ought to be dunked in sheep-dip."

As he picked up her sun-dried sidesaddle Phaedra dimpled up at him to brazenly demand, "Aren't you glad you let me come along? I managed to come just before you rolled off me just now, you brute. Do we have time to tear off just a little quick one before we have to ride on?"

Longarm laughed and said, "You'll pay for that remark, me proud beauty. But not just now. Lord knows how far ahead of us the others might be."

As he saddled her mount for her, Phaedra asked, "Are they really headed for that Mesa Verde I've heard so much about?"

To which he could only reply, in all honesty, "I don't know. We'll ask when we catch up. Can you really hit anything with that girlish little pistol you've been packing, honey?"

She hesitated, sighed, and told him, "Anything I can see to aim at. I'm quite a fair target shooter with me specs on. But since they fell off in that perishing river I've barely been able to make sense of anything ten yards away, and I wouldn't bet money on my hitting anything closer!"

Chapter 10

They cut sign a mile and a quarter to their southwest. It was plain enough for the nearsighted Phaedra to see a heap of horses had passed that way, albeit Longarm alone could make out shod or unshod hoofprints where the dry surface betwixt the sagebrush and creosote bush was fine-grained enough.

He made it six sets of shod hooves and eleven ponies running barefoot. It wasn't easy. The hoof marks tended to tangle, and the soft but persistent air currents at ground level didn't help. But whether he was counting the five shod ponies he knew about or six, meaning one of the owlhoot riders, all the shod prints overlaid the fainter sign of those ten to twelve unshod ponies.

When he said as much, taking time out to water their own stock, Phaedra asked just what that meant.

He shrugged and said, ''Means most if not all the critters Malone and his boys are chasing could be Indian ponies.''

As he remounted she declared, ''That horrid nudist who killed those two poor men while his confederates robbed our coach was undressed like an Indian, wasn't he?''

Longarm heeled his bay after the long-gone riding stock, with the sidesaddled English gal beside him as he told her, "Not exactly. He was wearing a Hopi ceremonial mask in Ute country, covered with South Sea Island tattoos. I already told you that one adds up to a vicious drunk from New Zealand. I don't know why the rest of his gang admire Mex duds and Indian ponies. But I mean to find out. In the meantime it's best not to sketch too detailed a picture out of thin air. Some say Billy the Kid has surprised so many older gunslicks, down Lincoln County way, by not fitting the picture they had of him in their heads. A gun hand out to take such a famous quick-draw artist can be thrown off his timing when he's suddenly face-to-face with a harmless-looking illustration from *Tom Sawyer*. It's best to keep an open mind and your eyes peeled for anybody who looks like anything when you're on the trail of armed robbers."

As they rounded a heavy clump of scrub he pointed at the sandier stretch ahead, where the hoof marks fanned out a mite, to elaborate, "We never pictured so many of the rascals, to begin with. You and those Mormon ladies only saw the one rascal in his birthday suit and that kachina mask. Your Jehu, Lem Redfern, only described a couple more in vaquero costume. None of you said you'd seen any horseflesh, shod, unshod, or flapping wings. So, starting out from Durango, yesterday, we figured we were looking for three or four of the rascals, with one of them likely wounded after that second brush along that same stretch of wagon trace."

He pointed at the trampled soil ahead to add, "Now we don't know what to think. But whatever we're tracking seems to be headed for the Mesa Verde, like Kevin Malone suspected they might."

Phaedra peered anxiously ahead with her beautiful half-useless hazel eyes as she exclaimed, "I wish I hadn't lost me bloody specs. I can make out the blue sky and what

83

seems a fuzzy flat horizon. I don't see any great green table."

Longarm answered soothingly, "Neither do I, albeit *some* of the Mesa Verde would have been visible to your right as you passed it in your coach the other day. The horizon to the southwest of here looks flat because it *is* flat, sort of. All the mesas in these parts are left over from what used to be the flat bottom of a mighty inland sea. Millions of years worth of occasional rains have carved a heap of this Four Corners range down to a lower level of the harder layers we call rimrock, leaving mesas, buttes, and such eight or ten stories up in the sky, whilst new canyons are cut through this new base level to turn all *this* into islands in the sky someday."

She insisted they ought to be able to *see* the one called the Mesa Verde if it was eight or ten stories bloody up.

He explained, "It's too big to take in all at once from any place in particular. You compared it a few days ago to that famous Manhattan Island they built New York City on. Nobody doubts it's an island, once they're *told* it is. But if we were *there* this afternoon, riding along any shore of said island, without a map to tell us just where we were, how would we *know* it was an island, not just one side of a river, from any particular spot?"

She tried to come up with an objection. Then she nodded soberly and said, "I see what you mean. Back home, you have to take it on faith that London is the biggest city in the world. There's no one place in London from which you can *see* it all at once!"

He stood in his stirrups to verify the distant gleam of sunlight off rippling water as he replied, "There you go. Like I told you back in Durango, the Mesa Verde ain't even properly mapped yet. It just sprawls out, over yonder, surrounded by lesser mesas great and small. We got to ford the Rio Manco to reach the canyon fans of that swamping mesa on the other side. So let's hope the ford upstream at that relay station ain't the only one!''

It wasn't. They followed the bewilderment of tracks across a sage flat and down an alarming clay bank to swirling muddy water that only wet the bottoms of Longarm's longer stirrups. Phaedra didn't have trouble with her spare pony this time. They forged up the far bank. The sign they'd been following still led toward the now more impressive sandstone cliffs of the Mesa Verde. Way down yonder a whispy chalk-line of wood smoke rose against the tan cliffs and cobalt blue sky. Longarm thoughtfully hauled the borrowed Winchester '73 out of its boot and levered a round in the chamber, saying, ''Somebody has lit a coffee fire, well this side of them cliffs. I want you to hang back at least a pistol shot as we drift in. I'm almost certain that has to be our side, unless the other side just dry-gulched 'em all.''

She asked, ''What do you call a pistol shot and what's a dry-gulch?''

He smiled thinly and explained, ''Fifty yards is about as far as an average shot can hit you for certain with a pistol ball. We wouldn't be able to talk to one another if you rode a *rifle* shot back. We call sniping from ambush dry-gulching because the best cover for a killing out on open range is most often a dry-gulch, and you get heaps of dry gulches here in canyon country. Now fall back, like I said, and when you see me get blown out of this saddle ride like hell up the Rio Manco for that relay station. Do you recall it from your coach trip west?''

She reined in her pony, saying, ''Of course. It was the last place we stopped to change teams before that robbery.''

He muttered, ''There you go,'' and rode on, the primed Winchester across his thighs with his right hand fixed to fire it, if need be.

But as they neared the small afternoon cooking break Longarm saw he'd guessed right about who'd been sending

85

up that smoke. Deputy Malone and the others hunkered around the fire rose when the rider they called Chinks spotted Longarm and Phaedra coming in and said so, loud. Their ponies had been tethered upwind of the fire, barebacked, as if Malone had planned to set a spell.

As Longarm emptied the chamber of his saddle gun and put it back in its boot he called Phaedra in, assuring her they'd caught up with the right bunch. As the two of them reined in to dismount near the bunch, Longarm asked how come, observing, "No offense, but there's still some daylight left."

Deputy Malone grimaced and replied, "I'm pleased as punch to see neither one of you got drownded, after all. But I'd rather you hadn't brung Miss Thorne out here. We got enough on our plate, no offense, Miss Thorne."

Longarm helped the little brunette down as he asked the deputy from Durango to fill them in a mite.

As a heavyset posse rider called Skinny rustled up some coffee for the new arrivals, Malone said, "We were about to give up, back at the scene of the crime, when old Chinks, there, found a busted padlock atop the rimrocks. Figuring it had to be from that strongbox, we circled farther than we might have 'til we come upon the tracks of one rider. We naturally followed 'em. They joined up with others, a *heap* of others. We make it a gang of a dozen, all told."

As Skinny handed Phaedra and Longarm their tin cups, the authoritative Chinks blustered, "*You* all made it out a dozen riders, you mean. This child ain't betting his honest wages on any such thing! I still say a single rider rode away from that road cut aboard one shod pony. Then he came upon the tracks of some wild mustangs and trailed after them in hopes of confounding any trackers, which I'd say he's done pretty good!"

Malone smiled tolerantly and turned back to Longarm to continue, "Them wild ponies Chinks is so certain of stuck together and forded the Rio Manco to some purpose. We

86

followed them this far. Then we saw where they seemed to be headed and decided to wait here for more help to show up. I'd sent Dave Wells back to town as soon as we saw how many we was after."

Longarm nodded and said, "That's how we knew where to find you all. You say you know where those others went?"

Malone pointed at the jumble of vertical sandstone pillars and clefts a mile or less on, saying, "The tracks lead direct for that Mesa Verde. Which of a dozen canyons they might have chose is still up for grabs. Riding any closer, with even one rifle hand up on the rimrocks, could take years off a man's life!"

Longarm sipped some strong black joe as he swept the skyline with his gun-muzzle-gray eyes. Malone had a point. The juniper and pinyon that gave the Mesa Verde its name rose above the sandstone crests as a spinach-green haze that could hide a multitude of sinners.

The blustering and hence annoying Chinks insisted, "Ain't nobody up none of them canyons but wild mustangs. They was running in a tight bunch because their boss stud *made* them stick together. That's how a boss stud herds his women and children. They've been grazing over to the far side of the Rio Manco. Now that the spring grass has commenced to summer-kill he's led them to greener pastures over yonder."

The posse leader asked Longarm what he thought.

Longarm moved past the fire toward the distant cliffs, his cup in hand as most of them trailed after him. He hadn't said Chinks was right or wrong, but the part-time deputy and full-time cowhand insisted in an injured tone, "Answer me this, if I'm so stupid. Answer me how come we read horseshoe sign as far as the Rio Manco and only unshod sign from the ford to this far?"

Malone said patiently, "I told you back yonder by the ford, old son. That one cuss parted company with his pals there. He rid into the shallow water, turned up or down-steam, and came out somewheres else.''

Chinks protested, ''How come? How come we picked up the trail of one rider near that busted padlock, followed it to where it commenced to follow a herd of wild mustangs, and then followed the fool mustangs after we lost that one cuss entire!''

''Longarm?'' asked Kevin Malone uncertainly.

Longarm moved on, saying, ''Works both ways, this far. There's a road agent out California way called Black Bart who may well be working alone and just pretending to have others backing his play from the cover all about. But eye-witnesses have testified to seeing more than one but way less than a dozen stopping stagecoaches in these parts.''

By this time they were well clear of the temporary camp, and the hoof marks leading on toward the Mesa Verde cliffs could be taken for those mystery ponies alone.

Chinks was grousing, ''We're way across the county line, into neither incorporated nor properly mapped wilderness. This child ain't about to chase wild horses through an endless maze, Malone!''

Longarm made no comment as he ambled on. Chinks was right about them being well west of the county line. He could be right about wild horses. The local Ute hadn't been given much time to pack when they were evicted from these parts and, like other horse Indians, they'd tended to tolerate wild or half-wild herds on their hunting grounds as a sort of informal remount service.

He spied some horse apples out ahead. He'd been spying the same all the way from Durango, for horses, cows, and other grazing critters shit more often and more casually than cats or dogs. But those turds ahead were the first he could say for certain had not been dropped by critters working for the stagecoach line or the La Plata County Sheriff's Department.

He finished the last of his tin cup and held it out to

Phaedra, asking her to hang on to it a second. Then he busted off a chaparral twig and hunkered down to bust a big fresh turd in two. He speared one half and raised it to his nose as Phaedra gasped, "Custis, that's rather disgusting!"

He sniffed, held the exposed inner working of the dung up to the light, and replied, "No, it ain't. The critter who dropped this grazed nothing but grass in recent memory. You got to grain-feed a horse or a mule for it to produce really stinky droppings, or enough endurance to matter."

Chinks said triumphantly, "I told you all we were tracking wild stock! That one cuss mounted up right followed them same mustang tracks to the river and lost us there, deliberate!"

Longarm tossed the speared turd aside and rose to full height as Malone griped, "We'd never get back there in time to scout both banks each way before sundown. He could have rid most any direction, for quite some time by now!"

Longarm took the empty cup back from Phaedra Thorne as he quietly remarked, "Miss Phaedra here and me might have met up with him. Have any of you gents ever met or heard tell of an unemployed hostler who calls himself Mike Dumont?"

Nobody there had.

Longarm swore under his breath and decided, "We'd still be looking for you all if we'd made him ride back to the stagecoach ford with us. He said they'd vouch for him. He could have been telling us the truth and still left them shod tracks that vanished at that other river crossing. He said he'd asked them for a job at the relay station. He might have. They'd say he had if he had, whether they'd ever seen him before or not."

Kevin Malone looked so sheepish that Longarm added, "Of course, I could be wrong. Mike Dumont could be the innocent saddle tramp we took him for. You can't take nothing for granted before you know for sure."

Malone sighed and said, "We just have time to make it up the river to the Widow O'Flynn's relay station. She bakes a mean meat pie, and it ain't easy to flimflam old Caitlin O'Flynn. We'll know by the time we set down for a swell supper whether she and her station hands really know that Dumont cuss or not!"

Nobody there had any call to argue with the leader of the posse. So they all headed back to the fire, with the bossy Chinks declaring they'd best saddle the most rested stock to consider serious riding in the time they had to work with.

They perforce followed his good suggestion, whether they were happy about his shouting it as an order or not. Chinks seemed to be one of those "natural leaders" who figured where the mob was headed and then ran out ahead of it.

They broke camp, mounted up, and rode north perhaps a furlong when a shot rang out behind them, and everyone who looked back saw the same cotton ball of gun smoke rising above the rimrock above that canyon mouth. Then the distant dry-gulcher fired again, and they were all tearing through the chaparral at full gallop. For it didn't require Chinks to yell it. They all knew their only chance was to get out of range as that rascal up yonder sent round after buffalo round after them, down here where they simply had no decent cover!

Chapter 11

Less than a mile on they came to an east-west dry wash
and got themselves and their ponies down in the natural
trench before old Chinks could order them.

Dismounting with saddle gun in hand, Longarm scrambled back up the south clay wall of the wash to prop his
elbows and the Winchester over the edge, betwixt two
clumps of silvery sage. He could see the cliff tops fair
enough from ground level. But the now more distant rifle-
man had ceased fire and just didn't seem to want to wave
at anybody wondering where he might be, up yonder.

Malone and Chinks joined him, one on either side. They
didn't know where the son of a bitch was either, but both
were full of notions about him.

Chinks said sportingly, "I was wrong. They must be Indians, or a dozen white men mounted on Indian ponies. We
must have 'em trapped in a box canyon. That's why that
one rascal was shooting at us before we could get any
closer, see?"

Longarm said, "I'm afraid I don't see, no offense. If I
was boxed in a blind alley and had a fistful of ammunition

and any hair on my chest I'd be delighted to wait for no more than seven riders, one of 'em a gal, higher up and firing from cover. I'd never let 'em know in advance I was waiting on 'em like a crafty spider. I'd let 'em ride in and pick off at least a couple before they knew I was there!''

Malone said, ''You're an experienced shootist with a rep, Longarm. What if we're dealing with scared kids? Or what if that one with all them tattoos is as loco as he looks? Or what if . . .''

''What if the Czar of all the Russians has conspired with Queen Victoria to interfere with the U.S. Mails?'' Longarm cut in. Then he added in a milder tone, ''I was asking questions, just now, not offering answers. Let's stick with what we know for certain. We know we've tracked a dozen or so unshod ponies as far as yonder canyon mouth. None of us knows how many of 'em were carrying riders. If *we* left Durango with spare mounts to switch to, there's nothing engraved on granite saying there was a rider on every one or even most of them other ponies. So what answer does that give us?''

Chinks didn't hesitate. He said, ''We know there's no more than a dozen but at least *some* damned outlaws boxed in that damned canyon!''

Longarm shook his head and pointed out, not unkindly, ''We don't know that at all. We know about a dozen sets of pony tracks lead in to a canyon that might or might not lead nowheres. We know somebody with a rifle gun is up on the rimrocks above said canyon, acting odd as all get-out. Why did he open fire as we were fixing to *leave*? Is that any way for a crafty spider in a corner to act?''

Chinks tried, ''Malone could be right about scared kids. Say one took some time to work up to the top. Say he blazed away as soon as he got there and saw us closer to the base of his cliffs.''

Kevin Malone, who'd proven to be a slower and more careful thinker, decided, ''He wanted us to move back and make more room, which we've done for him. Leaving the crowned heads of the Old World out of it, that has to be a box canyon because they wouldn't feel trapped over yonder if there was another way out. They don't dare make a break in our direction by broad day. They'd want some distance betwixt themselves and our guns if they meant to break out tonight, after the sun goes down and the moon ain't riz. That's the only way it works, gents!''

Longarm glanced up at the late afternoon sky as he considered the other lawman's words. Then he nodded grudgingly and said, ''No way we can work our way close enough to hit moving targets in the shades of evening without that son of a bitch up above hitting us. There has to be a better way.''

He fished a cheroot out of his vest and thumbnailed a light for it as he said, ''I'd offer, but we're far from town and I'm running low.''

Malone replied, ''I got my own, and by sundown we ought to have more riders out here with us. I sent to town for some.''

Longarm said, ''I noticed. Me and Miss Thorne never found you by pure guesswork. A few more guns to back our play don't make our play much better in them few vital hours before sundown and moonrise, this time of the month. Why don't you all hold this position, letting them know where you are, now and again, whilst I mosey west along this wash with my head and ass down?''

Chinks said, ''There's no way to circle that shootist high in the sky, Longarm!''

Longarm smiled wolfishly at the sandstone cliffs rising to their south as he enjoyed a drag on his cheroot, blew some smoke up for the edification of their distant observer, and said, ''Let's hope he thinks so too. Would you be kind enough to finish this smoke for me, Chinks? From up yonder they won't know for certain what they're looking at.

But smoke drifting through sage makes for shimmersome play of light.''

As he slid back down the bank, Malone called after him about another cook fire. Longarm said that sounded like a fine suggestion.

As he was headed for the riding stock to fetch that throw rope, he met Phaedra Thorne, who said, ''Oh, Custis, this is so exciting and I don't have either my sketch pad or my perishings specs to record all this desperate action! Where are you going, dear?''

He said, ''Fool's errand, if this wash don't take me far enough to the west. You stay here where it don't figure to get more desperate.''

He got the rope and forged on up the draw, making sure his Stetson didn't give his movements away to that distant sniper in the sky.

He didn't even try until he found himself alone at least half a mile off. Then he took off his hat and eased his bare head up betwixt some sage and soap weed. He couldn't make out that canyon mouth, for certain, from his new position. The north faces of the Mesa Verde were carved sort of complexicated by time and old *Waigon*, as you called the Thunderbird in Ho. That thick sandstone formation that extended all the way south into Navaho and Jicarilla country carved like brown laundry soap, albeit slower, to running water.

Where water ran mostly sideways the sandstone cliffs were undercut to form recessed shelves and overhangs. Where water ran straight down, the same stone was carved into vertical clefts, pillars, and such. That was the way the cliffs he was staring at were whittled by the weather. Pillars large and small stood out from deep shady clefts in the slanting afternoon sunlight. Longarm knew any secret admirers perched most anywhere up there amid the pinyon and junipers would be staring into sun-dazzle as they gazed his way. So he slid over the edge of the wash and commenced to snake-belly toward the bases of the cliffs through the chaparral, slow but sure as creeping lava. It took him an hour. Then he was too close for anyone along the rippled rimrocks to see him as he got to his feet and strode the rest of the way with more speed and purpose.

He found a cleft not too unlike the one he and Phaedra had followed to the top of that lesser mesa the night before. The way up was steepr and shorter this time. When he couldn't work any higher afoot he was able to rope a juniper branch jutting out over an edge above. Pulling hand over hand with the Winchester's reloading lever looped over one thumb and his boots planted against the gritty sandstone, he was soon atop the vast Mesa Verde. He'd have felt as if he was standing in a forest of dwarf trees if there hadn't been such an ass-puckering drop off to one side.

The thin layer of soil and evergreen duff underfoot muffled any sound of his cautious footsteps as he moved deeper into the elfin woodland and commenced to circle in toward that canyon mouth, hoping he was sure about where that might be. Then he heard a nasal voice softly singing that fool trail song about Pancho Bandito. As Longarm moved like lava through the dense cover, the cuss who seemed so happy about Pancho Bandito intoned,

"Pancho Bandito, alas and alack,
    Pancho Bandito got shot in the back.
    San Pedro, the angel, read off all his crimes,
    He sent Pancho Bandito to much warmer climes."

Now that he had the rifle hand atop the rimrock located, Longarm eased over to the edge *behind* the tuneful rascal. Peering over the edge into the shaded depths of the canyon, Longarm could see it ran back into the bulk of the massive Mesa Verde around a bend and out of sight from his point of view. He saw no sign of a camp or a single head of riding stock. A brushy wash wound down the center of the canyon floor, with clear rocky shelves up either side. The singing rascal to his north would know more about such details.

Longarm eased along the rim toward the ballad of Pancho Bandito until he made out the back of a lone figure in a big straw hat, brown *charro* outfit, and two six-guns. The cuss was holding a Spencer .52 like a guitar as he sang about Pancho shooting up Hell and complaining it was too cold.

Longarm quietly called out, "Drop that Spencer and grab you some sky, amigo mio. I got you covered point-blank with my Winchester."

Longarm's advice had been good and his tone had been mild. But all of a sudden the fool in the big hat had sprung to his feet to whirl around wildly, about a yard further out than the north rim of the Mesa Verde extended, aiming back, from way in the middle of the air.

He made that "Nnnnngggg!" sound a man might make in a dentist's chair as he dropped out of sight. Longarm made it over to the edge just after one awesome thud echoed off the canyon wall across the way. That big straw hat was still fluttering down, and down, to the dusty canyon floor.

Longarm peered over the rim at the tiny figure sprawled like a broken rag doll at the bottom of a stairwell and muttered, "That was dumb, kid."

He'd just had time to see the singing sniper had been a youth of, say, sixteen to twenty before that startled face had plunged out of sight.

Longarm moved over to the north rim of the natural buttress the kid had been holding against all comers, judging from the canteen and feed sack full of grub he hadn't taken over the edge with him.

Longarm stood tall as he was able and waved his hat higher until he spied hats waving back at him from that distant dry wash. Further off to the north, behind them, he spied dust billowing up in the late sunlight. As he saw the folk riding with him breaking cover to come on over he got his bearings and realized that had to be the stagecoach headed for Durango. It only seemed to be running a mite early because it *was* early, this far west. It still had to change teams at the Rio Manco and then the La Plata stations. That distant dust plume was the only sign of civilization betwixt this high vantage point and the far horizon to the north, dominated by the lonely purple mass of old Mount Hesperus, where the Thunderbird made his nest, according to the Ho.

So how come, Longarm wondered, had the outlaws hit that one coach twice so far from this fine lookout and hidey-hole? A beeline north to the lonesome wagon trace would give the gang way more time to fade back into the Mesa Verde by the time the coach made the extra fifteen miles or more up.

Longarm moved south to see if he could find the way that rifle hand had made it up here as he decided, ''Trying to make sense out of mean tattooed drunks and mean kids in Mex hats is like trying to figure out why skeeters wake you up with their whining before they bite you. Mean pests, by definition, act mean and pesky!''

Toting his own rifle and throw rope, he found another rope tied to a stout juniper trunk topside and running down into a cleft like a handrail. So he hooked his gun and gun arm through his own coiled rope, grabbed their rope with his free hand, and worked his way down to the canyon floor, fairly close to the mouth, about the time Malone and some others were gathering over the corpse of the singing wonder.

Longarm was glad they'd made Phaedra and the riding stock stay back, as he joined Malone and some men of stronger stomachs closer to the body. The Anglo youth in the Mex outfit had landed on his back. So his face was still there, albeit sort of flattened in the center of a wet halo of raspberry jam. Chinks asked Longarm what made him so mean.

Longarm said, "It was his own grand notion he could fly. Do any of you recognize what's left of him?"

Malone said, "Sure. Saddle tramp called Sterling Shaw. Got out of state prison earlier this spring. Looking for work around Durango, as I recall."

Chinks volunteered, "He asked out at our outfit. Ramrod wouldn't hire him as a cowhand. He admitted right out he didn't know how to rope."

Malone explained, "He came west with the railroad as a baggage clerk. Got fired when they caught him paying more attention to the baggage than the passengers liked. Last I heard, he'd applied over at the stage line. But they wouldn't have a known thief either."

Longarm stared soberly down at the sprawled body to observe, "I reckon he fell in with other bad company after that. I just had a look up this canyon, from up on the rim-rocks. There was nobody else to be seen, as far up as I could see. I'll be switched with snakes before I'll buy him guarding nothing at all with his life. Literal."

Malone glanced skyward before he decided, "This child would feel a whole lot safer if we commenced to explore the Mesa Verde bright and early. I just hate to be down in an unexplored canyon as the sun goes down. What do you say, Longarm?"

The more experienced lawman said, "If I was running things I'd post a lookout up where I just caught one singing and make camp a ways from this mangled corpse."

Malone grimaced and said, "Yeah, we'd best leave him where he is to dry. He'd only wind up messier if we tried to move him just yet."

He turned to Chinks to ask, "Do you reckon he'd cure just as dry if we pile rocks over him?"

Chinks shrugged and said, "As long as it don't rain. You

have to store 'em up under one of them deep overhangs if you want them to dry out and mummicate total.''

Longarm mildly inquired, ''What might you gents have in mind for this poor busted-up cuss? Did you say you aimed to *mummify* him?''

Malone nodded and cheerfully replied, ''He'll make a tidier and way lighter load when we have the time to pack him back to Durango if we let him dry out like all them cliff dwellers.''

Chinks made an expansive gesture at the sandstone cliffs above as he explained, ''There's something in the air, or mayhaps the rocks, up these Mesa Verde canyons. There don't seem to be no ruins here in this particular canyon. But back in '76, when old Bill Jackson and his expedition started to explore and photograph scientific, they found one dead Indian after another up behind them haunted houses, dried out like jerked beef amid all their clay pots and beads. They took most of the clay pots and beads home with 'em. Nobody would have all that much use for a mummicated Indian. But I understand they got a few in that Smithsonian Museum now.''

Malone snorted, ''I don't aim to offer the late Sterling Shaw to any museum. I just mean to let him soak in and dry out as he awaits our return to Durango. I understand the stage line has offered bounty money on the rascals who gunned Tom Cartier and Hiram Webber before they made off with a strongbox full of paper money.''

He nudged the soggy cadaver with a boot tip as he added, ''I don't aim to let the carrion crows and coyotes collect on him. Let's get some rocks and cover him good before we worry about where we'll have to spend the night.''

So they did. Then they made camp in the canyon's mouth with guards posted in turn up above to watch over them as they spread their bedrolls around the night fire.

It made Phaedra Thorne mad as hell. She'd been looking forward to nightfall all day. And now that night had fallen, she and Longarm had to behave themselves.

Chapter 12

The next day dawned dry and dazzling-bright. So after a breakfast of canned beans and dry biscuits dunked in black coffee, they moved up the canyon with a couple of riflemen covering them, afoot, from up amongst the greenery along the western top rim.

They found no sign of anyone, red or white, at first. There seemed little mystery about the lack of Indian sign. The local Ute had never cottoned to the Mesa Verde when they'd still held this quarter of Colorado, and the ancient cliff dwellers had dwelt along cliffs less open to the north winds and other unwelcome surprises.

Had not they tracked all those hoofprints into this blamed canyon they'd have had no occasion to suspect they were anywhere ahead for a mile or more. Chinks, out on point, spotted horse apples drying on the dusty bone-dry scree near the base of the cliffs. There wasn't enough dust to hold hoofprints as the canyon narrowed and grew ever less deep as they wound up it toward the forested top.

Riding back with Phaedra, Longarm told her, "I wasn't there. But I understand the old-time cliff dwellers hunted on top of the mesa and raised beans, corn, squash, and such in the canyon bottomland. I can't speak much for the ones who lived in these parts. But I've seen tolerable irrigation works in some dry country to the southwest.''

She asked what the former inhabitants of this semidesert had been called.

Longarm shrugged and said, ''Nobody can say what they called one another. Na-déné speakers of today call 'em Anasazi. Ho speakers call 'em Hohokum. The professors who study ancient ruins figure they lived up the sides of cliffs about the time King Richard the Lion Heart was crusading in our own Holy Lands. They only lived up cliffs a few generations, judging by their graves and garbage heaps. They were long gone two hundred years before Columbus made that wrong turn on his way to India. So us white folk can't be blamed for picking on *that* bunch of Indians, praise the Lord.''

She asked, ''What do you suppose happened to them?''

He had to confess, ''I don't know. Unlike some, I'm willing to admit I don't know. Some say they were wiped out by some plague or overrun by more ferocious tribes. But all the mummies and more bony remains that anyone's found appear to have been buried or stored away in back rooms formal, with their personal belongings and even toys, one at a time. Dead bodies pile up less tidy during the panic of plague or war. None of the ruins, so far, show any sign of siege or house-to-house fighting neither. They're a tad run-down, as you'd expect any housing to be after standing there empty for, say, five hundred years. But they look as if the folk living in 'em had simply moved away.''

Being a newspaper gal, Phaedra naturally wanted to know where the ancient cliff dwellers might have moved to.

He said, ''Like I said, I wasn't there. Of all the guess-work I've heard tell or read about, I like the notion they never moved all that far. The modern Pueblo Indians, speaking different dialects but all living much the same, build much the same style of housing and grow much the same sort of crops. I suspect their ancestors lived in way smaller villages up the side of cliffs, in smaller numbers, until they grew strong enough to build more spread out, on flatter land, and give up all that mountain climbing to and from the family cornfield.''

She asked, ''Aren't there any differences between the architecture of the long lost cliff dwellers and your modern Pueblo Indians?''

He answered easily, ''Sure there are. Do we build the same sorts of houses as our ancestors built five hundred years ago? Ain't there big stone castles back in England, where you hail from, and ain't none of your lords and ladies moved to more fashionable quarters since? Nobody ponders the mystery of the long lost castle dwellers of the British Isles, do they?''

She laughed and declared she'd already noticed he preferred to take the most practical approach to life.

He hoped neither the pudgy kid called Skinny up ahead, nor the tall drink of water called Spud behind them, were paying that much mind to the way Phaedra prattled on.

The canyon petered out, or perhaps began, in a network of shallow washes winding across the tree-covered top of the mesa. All they'd ever seen of those horses were widely scattered turds and what could have been hoof scrapes on the dry rocky trail that seemed to lead out across the mesa.

The bossy Chinks declared, and few could argue, that they hadn't had those ponies trapped after all. Chinks swept the shimmering green view all around with his free arm, bitching, ''Whether there was a big or little bunch riding 'em, or no bunch at all, they had all night and a fair slice of yesterday to run off most anywhere! These thick woods spread more than eighty square miles, and there's nothing to tell us they're *anywhere* up here instead of halfways to Mexico by way of yet another canyon!''

Malone said they'd rest up and have some more coffee on the notion. After he'd dismounted and tended to his and Phaedra's stock, Longarm took a leak out in the woods, smoked a cheroot, and jawed some as they waited for coffee to brew in the cooler boiling water at that altitude. He drank some damned coffee to clear his damned head before he grudgingly agreed the trail was cold down this way, whilst another two stagecoaches would be unprotected on that wagon trace to the north by the time they could get back to Durango, if they started now.

But then another posse rider, who'd been pissing off in another direction, returned to the fire to declare he'd picked up the trail some more. So they cussed him, made sure the fire was out, and let him take the damned lead.

The horse apples and other sign he'd come across led down into a shallow wash that kept getting deeper, then deeper, until they saw they were descending into another canyon, this one trending eastward toward the Rio Manco.

Longarm wasn't surprised when, rounding a bend, he spied what seemed a pueblo village running like books on a shelf along a higher overhang, carved out of the sandstone when the canyon-cutting waters had been running wider along a higher bottom.

The sunrise-facing alcove was a good place to build, if you were a cliff dweller by preference. This canyon was more fertile, with the wild cherry, box elder, and cottonwood growing almost to the rising sandstone cliffs. There was enough soil betwixt the tree boles to read the sign of unshod ponies, heaps of unshod ponies, moving down past the ruins, Indian file. But of course they reined in for a look-see, being members of the naturally curious human species.

The cliff dwellers who'd moved away had taken their notched log ladders with them. But brush that cliff dwellers never would have put up with had sprouted from the cracks below their ledge. So nobody but their visitor from London had much trouble working up the steep forty feet to the ruins, and Phaedra had Longarm to haul her up after him.

Once topside, they found themselves in a complex of terraced plazas and haunted houses. So, like kids, they spread out to play hide-and-seek with long gone Indians and possible outlaws. Albeit Chinks was certain, and most agreed, a gang would be dumb to hole up with solid rock behind and above them when they had all that open country to get away to.

Whether by accident or unconscious design, Longarm found himself alone with Phaedra amid the roofless back rooms of what might have been an extended family, way back when. Phaedra suddenly clutched his left sleeve and swung him around to dimple up at him and husk, "There's nobody else around right now, Custis!"

He said, "I noticed." Then he kissed her, but added, "Great minds run in the same channels, honey. But we might not be back here in private all that long. I'd sure feel silly if any number of the others caught us *in flagrante*. That means in the act."

She swore under her breath and said, "I know what *in flagrante* means, you big silly. I just want to get *in flagrante* with you because after a night without it I'm absobloody-lutely gushing for a good screwing!"

Longarm gulped, grinned, and murmured, "Gee, Mom, I thought she was a *nice* girl. I reckon that's what I get for teaching her to smoke three-for-a-nickel cheroots."

Then he kissed her again and murmured in a less mocking tone that it might be best to wait until they could screw more privately.

She clung to him, pleading, "Can't we just tear off a quick one, up against one of these stone walls? Can't you find us a cave or something, dear?"

He protested that any number could doubtless find the same niche as they explored the same ruins, even as he led her through a low keyhole-shaped doorway into gloomier light beyond.

She laughed and said, "Ooh! Spooky! Where are we, Custis?"

He told her, "Back of the inner walls, closer to the bare rock as it slants down to meet the natural shelf layer. The folk who used to dwell here seem to have used the otherwise useless notches behind their back walls the way we use cellers. Some were tidier housekeepers than others. So there's no saying what you'll find in odd nooks and crannies. Watch your feet as we work along the back wall a ways."

She followed willingly, murmuring, "See if you can find a place we can do it lying down, or dog style, at least!"

The best place he could find was a sort of alcove formed by the corner of the wall they were following giving way to another wall that hadn't been built quite as far back. He saw nothing but pitch-black darkness beyond. He swung Phaedra into the angle with the back of her broadcloth riding habit to the masonry and unbuttoned his frock coat and fly as they kissed again, hotter.

There was much to be said for the modest long skirts of the times. She hadn't been wearing anything under her own. So once she'd hooked one thigh over his forward-facing pistol grips, balancing on her left leg as she hauled his old organ grinder out, he only had to plant his own feet wider to run it up into her old ring-dang-do, and she hadn't been lying about how wet and wild she'd been feeling.

She came ahead of him, then climaxed a second time as he shot his own overnight accumulation of lust into her. They were still in that position, panting for breath as she throbbed around his shaft, when a bossy voice that had to go with those chinked chaps rang out in the gloom, "I heard somebody back yonder! Who's back yonder? I know you're back yonder, you sneaky son of a bitch!"

To which Longarm replied in as bossy a tone, buttoning

fast while Phaedra only had to lower her one leg, "Watch your mouth. Me and Miss Phaedra are exploring this sort of cave we just found!"

They heard Chinks and somebody else crunching through that keyhole. So he broke out his waterproof wax Mexican matches and struck a light just as Chinks demanded, "What are you two doing back here in the dark? You call that exploring?"

Longarm held the feeble light high, his voice steel-edged, as he softly replied, "When one match goes out you have to light another, and I ain't going to tell you again to watch your mouth, Chinks."

The bossy Chinks and politer but likely as suspicious Kevin Malone moved along the triangular passage toward them. Longarm was facing their way. So he didn't know what had made Phaedra scream like that until he turned her way, flickering flame near the sloped rock roof of the passage, to spy the same spooky sight.

A naked man lay curled up on his left side with his back against the sloping rock. His tawny skin was commencing to prune in the dry thin air, but you could see, even before Longarm struck another wax match, it was covered head to toe with curly South Sea tattoos.

"That has to be Seth Cooper, without that fool kachina mask!" the always bossy and often right Chinks declared.

Phaedra asked, "Is he . . . ?"

To which Longarm could only reply, "For some time. It's tougher to judge, where bodies tend to mummify instead of bloat. But he must have died soon after that new shotgun messenger blasted him, far way and more than two nights ago. So how in thunder did he wind up here, today?"

Chinks decided, "Easy. I can make out more than one buckshot hole from where I stand. He never come here. He was brung By them same outlaws we've trailed all this way. Dick Lloyd likely killed him on the spot, closer to the La Plata relay station. His pals didn't want us to find his

106

body. So they throwed it across a pack pony and packed it all this way to hide, here, where we just found it.''

Longarm moved closer, hunkered down by the body, and struck another light, informing the already wrinkled cadaver, ''Lord, you sure were one ugly cuss with your face all decorated as well. So why didn't they bury you closer to where you fell, or toss you in the Rio Manco so's the Indians to the south could worry about you, if they ever spotted you bobbing by in all that muddy water?''

The shot-up cadaver that only worked as that of Seth Cooper from New Zealand by way of Frisco and the Mormon Delta just went on grinning up at him until Longarm shook out the match to spare his fingers and rose back to his feet, saying, ''Makes no sense. But you got to believe your own eyes. He's starting to cure nicely, but, like that other one we buried to the north, it's going to take him longer to turn into a total mummy. Right now they're both still soggy, or worse, inside. So if I was running this show I'd leave 'em be for now and send a buckboard back from Durango to pick 'em up in a few more days.''

Herding everyone back along the passage Longarm added, ''The *living* members of the gang worry this child more. Neither that mean tattooed wonder nor the flying Sterling Shaw are likely to rob anybody anymore. So what say we push on and see if we can cut their trail again?''

Nobody argued as he followed them out through that same keyhole into way brighter light. As others gathered around to have Chinks lecture them on what he'd found hidden back in the rocks like a long dead pharaoh of Egypt Land, the more modest Deputy Malone took Longarm aside to quietly ask him, ''What was that about things making no sense? Miss Phaedra here and others reported a road agent answering to the description of a known outlaw called Seth Cooper. Lem Redfern and Dick Lloyd reported shooting at the same description with a ten-gauge, and here we have a buckshot-riddled body answering to the same description. So what are you asking for, egg in your beer?''

Longarm smiled thinly and asked, ''Have you ever had the feeling a fast-talking stranger with three walnut shells and a pea on a barrelhead was trying to mix you up?''

Malone confessed, ''I'm still confused about the last election. How could we have elected Rutherford B. Hayes when Sam Tilden had the most votes?''

Longarm told him sternly, ''Stick to crooks we have the powers to arrest. If I could tell you just what was bothering me, it might not be bothering me half as much. As I go over all that happened in my mind, all the *details* seem to make sense. But I can't fit them together as one sensible picture. I keep feeling I must be *missing* some parts of the puzzle.''

Malone snorted, ''Well, *sure* we're missing parts of the puzzle. We know Seth Cooper from New Zealand and Sterling Shaw from state prison weren't the only members of their gang. As to why either was behaving so *unusual*, why don't we ask the *other* members of their gang after we *catch* 'em?''

To which Longarm could only reply, ''When you're right you're right. Let's slide back down to our riding stock and ride on after the loco rascals!''

Chapter 13

Suppertime found them atop the wooded mesa after trailing scattered horseshit and even rarer hoof marks up and down many a canyon and over many a hill and dale in what appeared a wandering random pattern.

As they et around the juniper-limb cook fire in a clearing way up high, Chinks was holding forth again on his notion they'd been wasting time on a herd of wild mustangs. Longarm might have found it easier to agree if they hadn't left two dead outlaws drying out for later recovery along the way. The late Sterling Shaw had apparently been trying to keep them from catching up with those mysterious ponies.

When Phaedra suggested the poor lad might have been posted there to keep anyone from finding the already dead New Zealander, Longarm found her question too silly to answer, no matter how he felt about her in the dark.

Kevin Malone, across the fire from her, said, "That would be about as needlessly complicated as storing him on ice in Durango, ma'am. We could see Cooper had been dead at least a few days before we found him. So why didn't they just bury him if they were that worried about anyone finding him?''

The pudgy hand called Skinny volunteered, "Shaw must have been up there guarding against something else, Miss Phaedra. They only brung their tattooed pal along, dead or dying, and stuck him out of sight as easy on their backs as them old-timey cliff dwellers did it. State prison ain't filled with ambitious young gents who enjoy hard work and, speaking as an occasional posthole digger, I can assure you it ain't easy to dig graves in this country, betwixt rains.''

Longarm just blew smoke rings at the rising heat from the juniper coals, having no call to argue in circles like a fool pup chasing its own tail.

After dark he took Phaedra for a little after-supper stroll to settle their stomachs, together, off in the fragrant woods a ways.

She confided, over breakfast in front of others, that the friendly walk had helped her sleep more soundly.

They rode on, swinging widely through the dwarfed juniper and wind-tortured pinyon atop the big flat island in the sky. They found other sign, too much sign, of ponies roaming hither, yon, and all around Robin Hood's Barn. So along about nine Kevin Malone called everyone in to announce, "We're heading back to Durango. I don't know where those blamed outlaws wound up. I ain't about to waste more time tracking a scattered herd of wild or abandoned stock all over this blamed mesa!''

Nobody wanted to argue over that. Trail grub and sleeping under the stars *sounded* like more fun than it really was, and it wasn't as if they were only a spit and a holler from home.

Just getting back down off the Mesa Verde took some doing. They rode a good ways north to the wagon trace, and it was well after their usual noon dinnertime when they spied the Rio Manco and the relay station on the far side of the ford.

As they were fixing to cross over, Longarm spied what seemed like a big flat raft hauled partway up the far bank. It seemed to be made out of shorter planks nailed crossways to longer juniper poles. He asked Malone about it.

The local lawman said, "The late Rick O'Flynn from the County Wexford. He was always tinkering with something until he died from a sudden heart stroke and left poor Caitlin to manage the station in his place. Rick said he meant to build him a pontoon bridge across here so's the coaches could cross dry. Don't ask me why. As you see, he never finished but one float."

They crossed the shallow but boisterous Rio Manco the wetter way as the stage-line crew and what had to be the Widow O'Flynn came out of the 'dobe sprawl to wave them on over.

The four station hands were all kids. Three white boys and a breed. Caitlin O'Flynn made up for their nondescript impression by standing close to six feet tall in a blue denim smock and carrot-red curls. But her friendly face and ample curves allowed she'd enjoyed her life as best she could manage for perhaps thirty-five summers. A heap of her seemed to be muscle. When they were introduced she shook Longarm's hand with the grip of a gal who handled livestock for a living.

She cooked pretty good as well. It was easy to see Phaedra Thorne had some reservations about the older and way bigger woman's Irish brogue. Caitlin O'Flynn seemed to treat everyone with the same friendly but calmly-in-charge manners. When the pushy Chinks said he'd as soon have meat and potatoes for his free afternoon meal, the big redhead told him sweetly he'd have some meat pie or go hungry. So Chinks said he'd settle for her famous meat pie, and she said she should think so, considering her stage line was treating lawmen from another county and all so "dacent."

They were served out back on plank tables set up on the

111

shady side of the station, handy to the kitchen door.

Herself presided at the head of one table while her hired hands did the honors. Once the heavenly smelling meat pies were set before them, Phaedra was sport enough to dig in and pronounce the efforts of their Irish hostess a "delightful repast," to be answered by, "Garn and be after cutting your blarney, mum."

Longarm wished old-country English and Irish would quit talking that way to one another. He liked the big redhead, adored the petite brunette, and it wasn't his fight.

As they et he let Kevin Malone, talking plain American, bring the she-male station manager up to date on things, as far as they made a lick of sense.

Caitlin said she'd heard about both brushes with road agents from the coach crews passing through. She added, "I've a marvelous invention of Himself, the O'Flynn, to deal with any Tories bothering passengers around *this* station! But I doubt they ever will, us being so far west as the afternoon coach changes teams here and all and all."

Phaedra looked up from her delicious repast to demand, "*Tories* robbing your stagecoaches, Mrs. O'Flynn?"

The redhead laughed easily and explained, "I was speaking in the Irish sense, mum. I'd not be knowing why one of your English political parties chooses to be known as Tories. *We* mean it to describe a *pirate*, whether by sea or along the high roads of the auld sod. Tory is an island off our north coast, infested in early times by murtherous sea rovers. So I wasn't after insulting any fine English gintlemen when I called that gasoon in an Indian mask a Tory."

To change the subject, Longarm told Phaedra, "This far west of Durango, the gang would have to escape with the loot by broad daylight."

Then another thought hit him. So he added, "Ain't it dark, over this way, when them *night* coaches stop to swap teams, Miss Caitlin?"

The redhead said, "That it is, and who'd want to rob the

night coach coming from the east with heavy silver money in its boot and all and all?''

Before Longarm could answer, Malone said, ''The same bunch! Didn't they tell you about Redfern and Lloyd brushing with that loon in the kachina mask?''

Caitlin shrugged and said, ''They did indeed, and what good did it do the gasoons? Dick Lloyd shot one of them, and even if they'd gotten away with the strongbox, how far could they have carried it? *Smart* Tories are after paper money, as good as gold when it's time to be after the spending of it, but light as, well, paper, when it comes to the riding far and fast with it!''

Longarm washed down some meat pie with her damned fine coffee and said, ''I keep telling myself I'm missing something about this gang we've been hunting high and low for. I'd already noticed paper money in large or small denominations was way handier to ride with than a few hundred pounds of specie. Mayhaps they aim to spend their ill-gotten gains over in the Mormon Delta, where folk are old-fashioned about money. On the other hand, we don't have a thing connecting the late Seth Cooper from New Zealand with the Latter-Day Saints. He may well have started out as a total pagan praying to them tiki gods of the South Sea Islands.''

The topic of dumb stagecoach robbery was tossed back and forth until Longarm suddenly remembered he'd forgotten to ask about that rider from the west he and Phaedra had met along the wagon trace.

When he asked Caitlin O'Flynn what she could tell him about Mike Dumont, her only answer was a puzzled expression.

When he repeated the name neither she nor any of her hired help had ever heard of the cuss. After that, nobody recalled any rider who *could* have been that shabby stranger, asking for a job or just passing through, the other day.

Longarm smiled at Phaedra to drily ask, ''Does that surprise you half as much as it surprises me?''

The nearsighted English girl blinked her adorable eyes at him and answered, ''I don't understand. That man we met on the coach road the other day said he'd been here. He mentioned Mrs. O'Flynn by name and told us where he'd seen Deputy Malone and these others all around us!''

Longarm drily told her, ''Not exactly. So now I know what *three* of the outlaws looks like. Young Shaw and the tattooed Cooper are dead. But the lying rascal who flimflammed us with barefaced lies is yet to be accounted for, and I'll know him the next time I see him!''

Turning to Malone, Longarm explained, ''The one calling himself Mike Dumont rode a shod buckskin barb. He was likely the one leaving shod hoofprints for you riders, mixed in with the sign of that unshod stock. He split off, like Chinks here figured he had, further down the Rio Manco. He waded his mount upstream a ways, left the river where none of us ever got to, and catty-cornered to the wagon trace, where he stumbled over Miss Phaedra and me and, seeing I had the drop on him, lied his way past us by giving a false name and saying the folk here, who didn't know him, would be proud to vouch for him!''

Phaedra proved she had a nose for illustrated news by brightening and exclaiming, ''That's why he told us where we could find these chaps we were searching for! He didn't want us riding all the way in to this relay station to catch him in a big fat fib!''

Longarm smiled down at her to mutter, ''I just said that.''

Malone had been drawing maps in his own head. He volunteered, ''I see what you mean about trying to make the pieces fit. On the face of it, this mysterious Mike Dumont was headed back toward the scene of both crimes, after letting us trail him clean out of our proper jurisdiction. Old Chinks, here, was likely right about him, Sterling

Shaw, and the dead or dying New Zealander following a herd of wild mustangs to throw us off. But how come that fool kid in the Mex outfit was guarding that canyon mouth if there was nothing up it but stray stock?''

Longarm shook his head and said, ''You don't ask stock to stray the way you want to ride. You rope the herd stud and *lead* it the way you want all his wives to go.''

Chinks objected, ''Sterling Shaw didn't know how to rope.''

Longarm nodded but pointed out, ''We don't know how well the one we met as Mike Dumont might rope. He sure *lies* good. There could have been a few others with them. No matter how they managed it, they left a plain trail over to that maze of canyons, split up, and let the bulk of the herd drift onward and upward, leaving us too tangled a trail to mess with.''

Chinks, looking mighty pleased with himself, said, ''I knew that all the while. But how come that saddle tramp, Shaw, pegged them shots at us to keep us from making total asses of ourselves?''

Longarm said, ''He never. If you'll think back he only opened up on us as we were fixing to *turn away*! They wanted us to ride up that canyon and busy ourselves with the Mesa Verde for a spell, which we done. My getting the drop on Sterling Shaw and scaring him over the rim of the canyon wasn't part of their plan. His orders were doubtless to entice us good, then fade away through them woods atop the mesa and rejoin his pal or pals somewhere else. I'm still working on where that somewhere else might be.''

Malone said flatly, ''Durango. To catch that night train east over the divide with the money they've stole so far. They messed up with Redfern and that new shotgun messenger the other night. Their cannibal clown, leader, whatever, got shot by a better gun than poor old Tom Cartier was. I suspect Cooper died on the way over to the Mesa Verde. They'll never be able to stop a coach with his wild

115

act again. They're fixing to quit whilst they're ahead, see?''

Longarm cocked a brow to ask, "Are you saying you figure they've *reformed*?''

Malone smiled back and replied, "Not hardly. But the next time they stop any money in transit it'll be somewhere else with some different approach. We never heard tell of kachina dancers prancing out of the chaparral to rob coaches until just recent. I figure that sly one who slickered you the other day used poor old tattooed Cooper as his tool when the crazy drunk approached him for a job. His quick talking with you and Miss Phaedra proves he thinks fast in the saddle. He mixed us all up with that crazy act of Cooper's. Then he mixed us up some more with them stray ponies and another saddle tramp he used as a tool to be used or cast aside as need be. He didn't care whether we caught that kid or not. He never told Sterling Shaw his real name or true plans.''

Longarm muttered, "I sure wish someone would tell *me* what he and any survivors might be planning next!''

Phaedra asked, "Why did they leave their dead gang member, Seth Cooper, so far from the place he was shot?''

Chinks opined, "That's easy. To get him far from the place he was shot. They didn't have time to bury him along the way. They'd likely used that cliff dwelling before to hide out in. So they shoved him in back to dry out and be taken for an old dead cliff dweller if anyone ever found him.''

Phaedra objected, "A mummified Indian covered head to toe with Maori tattoos?''

Malone said, "It wouldn't have mattered in the end. It don't tell us who the mastermind is, or what's on his mind. But I still say he's headed back to Durango. That's where he'd have recruited Sterling Shaw and likely that tattooed cuss as well. That's where somebody took a shot at you, Longarm, before you could ever meet up with their mastermind in the very flesh!''

Longarm grimaced and said, "A lot of good it did me. From the way I've been blundering you'd think they'd want me alive and well to keep up the good work!"

Caitlin O'Flynn had been listening instead of talking. A rare talent for anyone of any sex or hair color. So they all paid her heed when she suddenly decided that she might have seen the tattooed wonder they were blathering about.

She said an odd passenger had passed through earlier that same month, dressed in an ulster coat, wearing kid gloves, with his face bandaged over and all and all.

He'd volunteered without being asked that he was suffering from some dreadful rash he had to see some great doctor in Denver about.

She added, "Now that I'd be thinking back to our conversation, I don't think he spoke like he'd been American born. At any rate, no matter who or what he was, he was off to Durango by sundown."

Longarm drained the last of his cup and rose to his feet, saying, "That makes two of us. If I can't get there before that night train leaves there's always that telegraph line."

Malone, Chinks, and Skinny were first to chase after him. But in the end they all tagged along, pushing their ponies considerable.

Chapter 14

You'd never read it in one of Ned Buntline's Wild West magazines, but a cavalry column crossed country at a third the speed of a stagecoach, and cow ponies took longer. That was simply because said coach got a fresh team every fifteen miles or so. A good team, starting out bright-eyed and bushy-tailed, could lope downhill, trot on the level, and walk uphill without stopping, and get you to your next relay stop and change of teams in less than two hours. But the ponies Longarm and his pals had been riding since sunrise couldn't. They'd left the Rio Manco station around four P.M. and walked their mighty jaded mounts into the La Plata stop with the sun mighty low behind them.

They were served a late supper by old Ruby, out front, as they told the jovial Harry Bekins about that mysterious rider who called himself Mike Dumont. Bekins said nobody like that had passed within eyesight of the river crossing over yonder.

Phaedra was anxious about the drawings she'd left in the fat man's care. He assured her they'd been safely stowed in the tack room. She wanted to see them anyway.

118

Longarm rose and followed after them as Bekins led the little gal from the *Illustrated London News* around to the stables. Phaedra picked up the plank the drawings were tacked to and carried it out into the daylight as she complained, "I can't see without me bloody specs. Do they look all right to you, Custis?"

He allowed they looked about the same as they had when she'd tacked them down, a lot soggier. Some of her watercolors had bled a mite. But her pencil or ink lines had come through just fine.

As she proceeded to untack and stack the dried flat paper, Bekins suddenly said, "There's dust rising against the sunset sky. I reckon it's Redfern, Lloyd, and the coach from the west. They sure do seem to be *flying* this evening!"

As Bekins waddled back to the station, Longarm told Phaedra he'd just come up with a better plan.

He said, "If you, me, and, say, Malone can fit aboard that eastbound coach as it leaves here, we can make it on to Durango way faster than we'd ever ride there on them jaded ponies."

She said she was game and added a naughty remark about the hotel near the Durango rail terminal as the two of them drifted after their fat host.

They started walking faster when they saw the coach splash across the La Plata without pause and roll into the station yard with its passengers yelling out both sides and the shotgun messenger, Dick Lloyd, alone up above, holding the ribbons and booting the brake lever as he brought the team to a dusty stop.

Before anyone on the ground could ask what had happened, Lloyd called out, "We was robbed! They shot poor Lem off his seat like a crow-bird and made me toss down the strongbox! I had no choice. They had the drop on me and I had to consider our passengers inside!"

Said passengers consisted of four men dressed Mormon and a spinster lady who wasn't. As they all piled out, glad to be alive and safe after all, Kevin Malone and Harry Bekins helped Dick Lloyd down and began to question him. So Longarm drifted over to ask one of the passengers what she'd seen.

The spinster gal, it was easy to see why she was still single, told him it had all happened so fast it had been over before she and the men inside with her were certain anything was wrong. Their coach had paused at the top of a long grade. Then they'd heard shots, gruff commands, and the next thing they'd known they were off and running with their new driver shouting only a few details down to the Mormon gentleman who'd opened a side door and leaned out to ask what was going on.

Longarm thanked her and moved over to where Dick Lloyd was jawing with Bekins and Malone near the yellow front wheels of the mostly maroon coach.

Malone turned to Longarm to say, "They done it again. Same place they robbed this same coach earlier. So I reckon we don't want to head back to Durango just now after all!"

Longarm nodded, staring at the erstwhile shotgun messenger as he replied, "I reckon we don't. I see you're packing a S&W .45 on your hip and you would have had that ten-gauge across your knees at the time, wouldn't you have, old son?"

The lean and wiry professional shootist replied with an innocent but frosty smile, "They made me toss my Greener down with the strongbox. There were four of 'em, covering me from both sides of that gap atop that same rise. You would have done no more than I did. I have a fair rep, my own self. But I don't mind saying this child was sort of rattled by their blowing Lem away without any sensible reason I could see!"

Longarm answered soberly, "Oh, it's commencing to make a lot more sense. I know your rep, Lloyd. You say Lem Redfern drove up that same long slope this evening, without making the passengers get out and carry their baggage? Four men, one woman, and their baggage have to weigh more than three gals and one man did that first time, or could I be adding my rough figures wrong?"

Lloyd shrugged and said, "I wasn't there that other time. You'd have to ask poor old Lem about all that. If you could. Like I said, they just killed him deader than a turn in a milk bucket!"

"Like you said," Longarm purred ominously.

Dick Lloyd was a professional gunfighter with his gun in a tie-down holster. So he never waited for Longarm to accuse him outright. He went for his double-action .45, sure he could beat Longarm's cross-draw.

He probably could have. But just as the heel of his palm slapped the ivory grips of his .45 he stopped a .44 slug with his chest, and then he was staring in fascinated horror through the gun smoke between them at the bitty derringer in Longarm's big right fist as he slid slowly down the wheel behind him, staining some yellow spokes red.

Longarm swung the double derringer to cover Bekins as he told the bewildered Deputy Malone, "I sort of figured he might be that dumb. That was why I was holding this whore pistol, palmed. Now I want you and your riders to secure this station good! Arrest everyone but them passengers and line 'em all up by that plank table we just supped at. What are you waiting for? A kiss good-bye?"

Malone was in motion, yelling orders he wasn't too sure about, as Longarm held his derringer on the suddenly ashen fat man whilst he drew his revolver backward with his left hand and suddenly shifted to cover Bekins better as he quietly observed, "It ain't too late to turn State's evidence. You'll hang with them others if you don't and we both know you ain't killed anybody, direct."

Bekins licked his pink lips and protested, "Have you gone crazy? My crews and my stage line are the *victims* of those road agents. Not the road agents who killed Tom Cartier and that passenger as well as poor old Lem! I was never anywhere near either robbery, and I can prove it!''

Longarm replied, ''I just said that. I ain't fixing to offer you a second chance to turn State's evidence. I don't have to, and I don't like you. But my boss has often told me to keep things simple, when and if I can. I want you to move on over to that table and set down with the others, now. Keep your hands polite and don't make no sudden moves. For to tell you the truth I'd love to drill through all that lard with some spinning .44-40 slugs!''

Bekins gibbered, ''You're crazy! I've never done anything to you or anybody else! I'm innocent as a babe and pure as the driven snow!''

Longarm frog-marched him over to join the others in front of the main building. The officious Chinks asked if there was anything he could take charge of.

Longarm nodded and said, ''You might disarm a couple of the station hands for certain and have them wrap that one body in a tarp. You'll be taking him on to Durango with you.''

Chinks asked, ''*We* will? Where are *you* fixing to ride, Longarm?''

''I ain't sure yet,'' Longarm replied.

Then he locked eyes with old Ruby, closer to the table, her brown moon face impassive as if she'd been standing out front of a cigar store. He nodded at her and pointed at the nearest doorway with his chin. She nodded, turned, and waddled inside.

He followed, and as soon as they were alone in the gloomy main room he told her, ''Say nothing until I say something important, *Umbea*. I know much about what's been going on out this way. I know you have been watching, and listening. I know you can tell me about the little I haven't figured out for certain yet.''

The no-longer-young and never-pretty Ute woman stared down at the floor between them to murmur, ''Harry has been kind to me, *Saltu ka Saltu*.''

Longarm warned, "I hadn't finished. Harry Bekins is fixing to hang no matter what you say or do. I feel for what this will mean to you. But I don't write the laws for us *Saltum*. They say a man who aids and abets a killer whilst he steals from his boss has to do the rope dance if he refuses to change sides before the trial and, so far, the fool keeps telling us he's innocent."

She covered her face with her apron and sobbed, "Hear me! Harry is not a wicked man. He is only greedy, greedy!"

Longarm said he'd noticed and continued, "The same federal laws that punish us *Saltum* severe for messing with the U.S. Mails consider folk like yourself wards of the state. If I was to turn you over to the Bureau of Indian Affairs as poor benighted heathen some white crooks took advantage of, they'd doubtless send you down to the South Ute Reservation and give you your own allotment number."

He could tell she was thinking his offer over. He let her, whilst he got out a cheroot and lit up.

He was still smoking it, five minutes later, when the two of them stepped back outside. He waved Kevin Malone over and tersely told the younger lawman, "I got me some hard riding to do. I ain't got time to talk. But Ruby, here, will tell you the whole tangled tale. After you get a better grip on the situation you'll want to make sure the westbound night coach turns around and goes back to Durango with everybody. Lock Bekins and his hands in your county jail, turn Ruby over to the BIA, and don't let nobody do anything else until they hear from me!"

Then he was legging it for the corrals, with Malone striding with him and Phaedra Thorne running after them.

As he roped and harnessed a fresh mule and led it over to the saddle and bridle he'd left to dry on a corral pole, both Malone and Phaedra badgered him for some answers.

He managed to explain that only the one elderly Mormon, the late Hiram Webber, had actually been murdered.

He said, "That was only because he horned in with his own gun. It was mostly a fool charade. One stationmaster and a few crooked hands knew the company and their insurance dicks would suspect an inside job if it looked at all like an inside job. So when they saw a sudden chance to pin it all on a known road agent, they jumped at it."

Then he'd saddled and bridled the fresh mule, mounted up, and just had time to tell Phaedra they'd talk about it some more at the hotel in Durango before he was out of the corral at full gallop, splashing across the La Plata and riding into the sunset for the Rio Manco as he used the barrel of his drawn Winchester as a quirt.

The fresh mule made better time than any spent pony could have. So it didn't take long to lope through that gap frequented by road agents, or so some kept saying. Longarm didn't waste time scouting for sign. He took advantage of the long slope ahead to lope the spunky mule.

It still took them the better part of two hours and, as they topped a rise a couple of miles short of the Rio Manco, Longarm saw to his dismay, albeit without much surprise, that the relay station run by the redheaded Widow O'Flynn was on fire and then some!

"Bastards!" he snarled as he gave his mule's rump a good lick with the Winchester to ride in at full gallop, doubting anyone who might be laying for him could still be there.

He saw he was right when the big buxom redhead ran along the wagon ruts to meet him, shouting, "Lem Redfern and the ghost of Tom Cartier! They tricked us! Lem hailed ahead in the gathering dusk, and we suspected nothing as they rode in. When I saw Tom Cartier with Lem, Tom being dead and all, I ran into the house for the grand invention of Himself the O'Flynn. But before I could do a thing they'd shot two of me poor lads and all of me mules, save for the fresh ones they were after riding off on! They even shot the ponies they'd been riding, the murtherous divvels! I don't know which of them set the station afire, or why!''

Longarm regarded the monsterous dragoon pistol in her big right hand, but didn't ask if chambering it to fire wrist-busting .54 rounds was her late husband's grand invention. He said, ''You're lucky they didn't kill you too. They're *both* supposed to be dead right now. If they figured their charade was commencing to fall apart, speed was of more essence. How much of a lead might they have on me and this one mule, Miss Caitlin?''

She said, ''Over two hours. They rode in not too long after the eastbound coach came through, with Lem, the divvel, driving!''

Longarm saw a surviving station hand hauling furniture out of the burning building. So he dismounted, Winchester in hand, and handed the reins to Caitlin, saying, ''Ride on to the La Plata station and they'll explain it all as they see you safely in to Durango.''

But she led the mule after him as he headed for the riverbank in the flickering light. She demanded, ''And would you be after chasing them two desperate divvels on *foot*, me darling avenger?''

To which Longarm could only reply, ''They just made certain I can't hope to overtake 'em along your long stage route. They'll ride your poor mules to the next relay station, pull the same dirty tricks, and be off on another pair of fast fresh mounts, all the way west to the Mormon Delta.''

He legged it up the bank to where that log float lay half in and half out of the swift current. He set his Winchester on the cross planks and bent to heave the dry end, experimentally. The big carrottop unlashed the bedroll and saddlebags from his borrowed roper and tossed them aboard as well, saying, ''There'll be divvel a general store where you'll be off to if it's a moonlight cruise you have in mind, me hearty!''

He said, ''Thanks. I ain't sure how long it's likely to

take. But I do know this river flows south to the San Juan, which flows west to meet up with the Colorado near that Glen Canyon ford.''

''With many a rapid and maybe a few waterfalls along the way,'' she pointed out. ''You're more likely to be after drowning yourself than overtaking them mounted villains aboard this raft, and who did you think you were, Tom Sawyer?''

Then she'd let the mule fend for itself as she hunkered down beside him to help him launch the raft, complaining, ''This is madness. Sure, I ought to have me head examined! We're nivver going to make it!''

Then the current caught the heavy logs and Longarm had to leap aboard before his only chance could get away. Her remark about ''we'' was still sinking in as she jumped aboard before he could tell her not to. He told her she was crazy as he started to unlash one of the steering poles to run them back to the bank. But Caitlin said, ''Push off for the middle if you mean to round the first bend. I know I'm crazy. I was just after saying I was. But didn't it sound like a grand adventure when Tom and Huck went rafting away togither and all and all?''

Chapter 15

The first few miles were scary as all get-out, with the float bobbing under them as if it had a mind of its own and might have been bent on suicide. The stars above looked close enough to scoop out of the black velvet sky with your hat, but the water dashing on all sides ran like coal dust through a coal chute, and when they bumped and swung or sailed over a submerged rock with the current, they could only hang on and hope the float knew what it was doing.

Then the moon rose above the mesas to their east, like a big lopsided Chinese lantern, and shed enough light for them to guess a tad better at their surroundings.

The high cliffs of the Mesa Verde loomed to the southwest as a ghostly stone wall as the moon's pale rays bounced back from the pale rocks. The river now looked more like shiny black ink, swirling south between black lace garter ribbons. Hunkered side by side near the saddle in the center, the both of them gripping steering poles they'd rustled up in the dark, Longarm and Caitlin agreed they were moving slower than by railroad but faster than by coach. She decided, "I'd make it ten miles an hour if you'd be after telling me what good this will be doing us. Them villains ain't riding southwest on me mules. They're beelining almost due west, and averaging nine miles an hour as they do so! It's simple arithmetic, Dipety Long. We've twice as far to go, and we're not going twice as fast at all at all!''

He rose to one knee with his pole as he spied an ominously slick patch of water ahead, saying, "Sandbar coming our way, or vice versa. If I've figured my basic trigonometry right we're only losing on them serious until we swing around the south end of yonder Mesa Verde, where the Rio Manco flows close to due west to join the bigger and swifter San Juan, which ought to carry us in the same general direction, faster than they can average by coach mule, no offense. They have to take the time out to raid and swap mounts every fifteen miles or so. We'll be moving steady with the current all the time. I doubt they'll chance hitting that big home station at Clay Hills. They'll likely try swinging around it, making for the Glen Canyon. That's where I'm hoping to stop them, if only I can get there first!''

She hefted the murderous rechambered six-gun her husband had rebored, saying, "The least you could offer me for the hire of this grand float would be one free shot at the mastermind. Which one might be the mastermind, by the way, and would you be after telling me what this is all about, now that we have the time?''

Longarm dug one end of his pole into the sandy bottom to steer them around the slick as he explained, "I knew something was wrong from the beginning because things just didn't add up sensible. I had a better grasp of the flimflam after they steered us into discovering the already drying out body of that tattooed fugitive, Seth Cooper. You don't gun two men, get shotgunned two days later, then run up a canyon dead or alive to dry out that much, that soon. After that, once we got back to Harry Bekin's tack room and I had a second look at some artwork for the *Illustrated London News* I recognized the flimflam man we'd met along the trail. The one who said he was Mike Dumont and that you'd vouch for him.''

She insisted, ''I was after telling you before sunset. I never laid eyes on the liar!''

Longarm poled them toward a swifter race near the middle of the modest river as he told her, ''Yes, you had. Only you knew him as Tom Cartier, the shotgun messenger Lem Redfern reported as a victim of the tattooed maniac in that kachina mask! Neither Miss Phaedra nor them Mormon wives who saw the naked wild man gun Hiram Webber really saw him gun Tom Cartier. They heard shots, saw gun smoke, and heard their driver *say* he was standing over poor Tom's body. Poor Tom and that rascal in the kachina mask with tattoos drawn all over him with ink he could wash off carried the strongbox away together, once the robbed coach had rolled on. They never carried it all the way over to the Mesa Verde. They could hide money anywhere, once they had that unexpected but welcome rain to hide any possible sign they might have left.''

The semiliterate immigrant gal asked dubiously, ''You figure all that out with this high school triggery, Dipety Long?''

He said, ''My friends call me Custis and they gave a war I had to go to before I ever finished high school back in West-by-God-Virginia. But as I understand trigonometry, it's the study of where moving things going different ways might meet up. Once I knew Tom Cartier hadn't been killed, after all, I figured it was suspicious of the shotgun messenger who'd replaced him to report the Jehu who'd reported him dead was dead as well.''

She blinked owlishly at him in the moonlight and demanded he go over that again.

He shook his head and said, ''It'll be easier to follow if I tell you what old Ruby over to the La Plata Station told me. I tried to get it out of Dick Lloyd, and he slapped leather on me. I tried to get it out of Harry Bekins, and he just went on flimflamming. So I made a deal with Ruby. She allowed she'd rather tell me all she knew than spend the rest of her days in prison, and it's surprising how much a Ute housekeeper and play-pretty can pick up as the men she's serving conspire as if she wasn't there.''

Caitlin said, ''I deal with strangers just passing through every day, and *you'd* be surprised at how freely some blather after a long coach ride and a fast snort of the creature. But what was that squaw after telling you, ah, Custis?''

Longarm said, ''In the beginning there was more talk than intent about that paper cash passing through their hands in considerable quantity. But they knew that they'd naturally be the first ones to be suspected, and currycombed for any loose change they couldn't account for unless they could make it look as if somebody else had done it.''

Caitlin used her own pole to ward her end of the oblong float away from a midstream boulder as she decided, ''An inside job *was* after crossing me mind, the moment I heard our eastbound had been robbed in Turner's Gap and all and all. I was ashamed of myself as soon as I heard poor Tom had been killed by the villains, though.''

Longarm said, ''That's how come they done it the way they done it. Ruby says that mysterious passenger you remembered, wrapped up in an ulster and bandages, was really Seth Cooper from New Zealand, and he was really suffering a dreadful fever. You wind up with such fevers from infected buckshot wounds. He got off the coach at La Plata, as if to relieve himself, and never got back on. Harry Bekins found him in a heap out back and sent Lem, Tom, and the other passengers on with the coach to Durango. He and old Ruby tried to nurse the feverish rascal. But he died on them, delirious, after blabbing at them about being wanted by the law, getting shot at over in the Mormon

Delta, and so on. Instead of reporting the death, they salted him down and had a saddle tramp who'd been pestering them for work run the body over to some Indian ruins Tom Cartier knew of, in a Mesa Verde canyon. The body was hid just good enough to be found, in time, by any serious lawmen lured up that same canyon. They knew hardly anyone can ride past a deserted homestead or haunted cliff dwelling without exploring it a heap."

She nodded and said, "I heard about the two bodies you left over by the Mesa Verde to be recovered later. I see how they faked Tom's death to make us all think the coach he'd been after guarding had been robbed by a desperate tattooed maniac wanted in other parts of this land. But why did they go through all that guff about a robbery attempt that never came off?"

Longarm said, "That was to set up their next moves. They wanted to establish an old pal, Dick Lloyd, as an honest employee above any suspicion, seeing he hadn't been working for the line during that first real robbery. He and Lem Redfern didn't brush with anybody as they drove through Turner's Gap in the dark. They just made a heap of noise and *told* the passengers a tall tale. Which the passengers repeated, as if they'd witnessed things that just hadn't happened."

Caitlin said, "Oh, me eyebrow, and to think I've served meat pie to both thim crooks without suspecting they could lie like an English moneylender! What happens next?"

Longarm said, "They suckered us. Almost, leastways. After the county possed up and I went along to play big shot, their plan was for us to spend days on a snipe hunt, decide crazy Seth Cooper, their leader or Lord High Executioner, had died of wounds received at the hands of the heroic Dick Lloyd, and, meanwhile, they'd stage another robbery, faking Lem Redfern's demise this time, leaving everyone on our side with no obvious suspects to consider. We weren't supposed to figure two dead men had ridden

131

off with the contents of two strongboxes. Anyone anybody had any call to suspect had partial alibies and none of the money on them. The plan was for the unfortunates killed by the mythical gang led by an established but *sincerely* dead road agent to make it clean out of these parts with the money, lay low, and wait for their cleared pals to come join them. Ruby told me there's been talk about abandoning your stage line as too long and carrying too little to be profitsome.''

Caitlin sighed and said she'd heard the same, adding, ''Sure I've ever wanted to see California, and Wells Fargo pays better on its Coast Range runs. But there's something I don't understand about the inside job they were after pulling off on the line I work for now. Why do you suppose they dropped all their pretenses and just rode off on me poor darling mules this avening? Wouldn't they have expected me to tell the whole world I'd just been robbed by two dead men, heading west like woild Indians?''

Longarm shoved his pole against another foaming boulder as he calmly replied, ''Ruby and me were talking about that. It's one of the reasons she felt more like talking. I took the more generous view that they bolted when they saw things had started to go wrong on them. We were supposed to find that tattooed corpse and other sign tying some gang of loco outsiders to the Mesa Verde instead of the stage line the real crooks worked for. But Miss Phaedra and me weren't supposed to meet up with the late Tom Cartier in the flesh. He knew she'd sketched his likeness not too long before. So she should have known who he was on sight. Then he noticed she was half blind without her glasses, while I'd never met him before. So he bluffed his way through us. But it must have unsettled him some.''

He probed for the bottom, found they were moving swift and sure down a deep channel, and continued, ''When his partners, Lem and Dick, stopped up at your place this afternoon with the coach they meant to rob at dusk, and you told them what you surely must have told them about us heading the same way, after giving up our snipe hunt sooner than they'd planned, they might have suspected we were on to more than we really were. The rest we know. They staged the fake robbery as planned, the deceased shotgun messenger pretending to gun the only survivor of the earlier robbery, then they lit out lickety-split to reach the Mormon Delta before anyone else could overtake 'em.''

As their float swirled around in an eddy but kept on downstream at the same speed, he added, ''Nobody following them on horseback, I mean. Ruby thinks they meant to double-cross her Harry and their confederates at the La Plata Station all the time. She said Harry came up with the grand design after that tattooed New Zealander died on them so private. She said hard words were exchanged, more than once, as to how the spoils should be divided among the merely cunning and the really brave. She doesn't think Lem and Tom are really headed for Salt Lake City, as agreed. I don't think so either, whether it's because they were planning a double cross earlier or happen to be aware we'll surely have wires out on 'em at every railroad town erelong.''

She asked where he thought the rascals really meant to hide out.

Their float went over some submerged rocks with an alarming lurch, with a sheet of muddy water washing across the planking as they tore sideways to the current. So he waited until he had them lined up with the Rio Manco and commenced to lash the saddle firmly to the planks before he replied, ''Can't say. It's a big country and they could go most anywhere with all that money to pay their way. That's why we have to beat them over to that Glen Canyon. We can't float up the Escalante against the current after them, and I'll never catch two mules on foot, uphill!''

Caitlin soberly pointed out, ''We'd never be after floating this soggy pontoon up the even mightier Colorado ei-

133

ther. If we make it to the San Juan, and the San Juan don't drown us on the way to the grander Colorado, they'll be crossing the Colorado more than ten miles up from where the San Juan empties into it! How in the divvel do you propose to get from the junction downstream to the crossing ten miles *upstream*?''

Longarm sighed and said, ''I reckon I'll have to leg it. My boots have low heels, and I can stride four miles an hour if I have to. But why not eat this apple a bite at a time? We've got over a hundred miles of brawling water ahead of us, dropping a country mile by the time we end up at the Colorado. You said yourself, there may be all sorts of rapids and worse ahead. So who's to say we'll ever make it all that way alive?''

She laughed wildly and declared, ''As mad as a hatter and brave as a lion and who ever wanted to end her days serving tea to safe and sane old turf diggers? This reminds me of when I first came west, with Himself, the O'Flynn. Me mathair warned me the O'Flynn would be the early death of me, and there was minny a toim I thought me mathair had been right. But it was a grand time we had, seeking our fortunes and enjoying the trying as much as we ever might have enjoyed the spending of it all and all.''

He allowed he'd headed west after the war from a life that seemed a mite dull after Shiloh and such. He said, ''I follow your drift about trying. I tried panning color, shooting buff, herding cows, and such before I finally wound up scouting for the army and riding for the Justice Department. I've never wound up rich. But then I've never wound up hobo-broke for long, and sometimes, topping a rise in the green up when the pasqueflowers are in bloom to the far horizon, you do get to thinking it's the riding there you enjoy as much as the getting there.''

The big buxom redhead heaved a mighty sigh and declared, ''Jasus, Mary, and Joseph, it's in love with another grand fool I'll be falling if you don't lave off that poetic blarney about woild flowers in the spring, in this moonlight too, ye woild deceiver!''

Longarm chuckled and held out a hand to her, saying, ''I'd as soon drown in such romantic company too.''

She took his hand in both of hers and pulled him over the saddle to catch him off balance in a bear hug and give him a swell kiss. But just as he got one leg over the saddle to keep them both from falling overboard as he kissed her back, Caitlin twisted her moist lips to one side and warned, ''That's enough, for now. We'd best be rafting down to the grand Colorado with our wits about us and save the auld jig-a-jig-jig for later!''

He had to allow her words made sense as he watched the swirling black ink ahead for rapids or worse.

He could only hope, as Caitlin O'Flynn manned that other pole in the moonlight, she'd meant what she'd said about later. He hadn't expected a gal that big and strong to kiss that sweet and tender.

Chapter 16

Before the moon was at the zenith they'd circled south of the Mesa Verde and swirled on through ever deepening banks to meet the bigger and brawnier San Juan just a few miles east of where those four corners of Colorado, New Mexico, Arizona, and Utah met.

The official benchmark stood on the high windswept range above them to their left as they whipped past in growing terror, with the moonlight uncertain on the swirling black water they were riding like toy soldiers on a kid's toy boat down a rain gutter.

They ran the merely frightening rapids and poled themselves ashore to work the heavy raft down the really bad runs with the long throw rope from that saddle.

They left the saddle lashed to the planking to take its chances with the float, but they naturally portaged the saddlebags and bedroll. So neither got soggy or lost the times the float turned all the way over in the boils at the foot of some serious rapids.

Between such bad patches the San Juan flowed swiftly but serene and only the movements of the overhead rimrocks against the starry sky let them know how fast they were moving.

Caitlin allowed she found their moonlight cruise mighty romantic. But it seemed every time they got to swapping spit, cuddled together in the middle with Longarm's damp back braced against the clammy leather of his borrowed saddle, they'd hear the ominous gurgles of another bad stretch ahead and have to forgo romance in favor of survival.

The Rio Manco had trended a mite to the south as it carried them mostly to the west. The San Juan swung them more to the north as it carried them faster toward the deeper canyon lands of the Colorado. When they spied beads of light above them on the north rim, Caitlin declared, "If that's the Mormon outpost I think it could be, we're making good time indade!"

Longarm got out his pocket watch, squinting hard in the moonlight, and decided, "It better be. It's after midnight. It's tough to judge aboard these soggy logs. I'm more used to traveling by train or in the saddle. This feels sort of in-between. We're likely going slower than it feels, though. Our main advantages are twofold. To begin with we're likely moving faster, constant, than a rider changing to a fresh mount every fifteen miles or so could average. We ain't walking this float uphill, loping it downhill, or trotting it anywheres. We don't pause on rises for even short breaks, and of course we don't waste any time changing to a new float every fifteen miles."

He fished out a cheroot to share with her as he went on, "In the second place, we're traveling more comfortable."

As he lit the cheroot Caitlin chided, "You're speaking in jest! Or else you have no feelings! It's chilled I am, with a wet rump and a growling gut and, if the truth would be told and we knew one another better, it's a piss I've been wanting to take for hours!"

He laughed and allowed he wouldn't peek whilst he

broke out some canned grub and unrolled the bedding, with the waterproof tarp on the damp planking. He could still hear the sibilant hiss as Caitlin squatted at the downstream end of the deck with her substantial rump hanging out ahead of them. He didn't comment when he heard a trout jumping or her crapping either. When she joined him on the spread-out blankets he handed her both the lit cheroot and an opened can of pork and beans before he rose, murmuring, "Great minds run in the same channels and I'd be obliged if you didn't peek either."

But as he enjoyed a good leak over the side with his back to her, Caitlin couldn't resist giggling and confiding, "It's just as well we're both country bred, and it's a grand hose you'd be after putting that fire out with! And what did that little stuck-up English girl have to say about it?"

He shook it off, buttoned up, and hunkered down to splash his hands in the water as he calmly replied, "Nothing. We were never forced to relieve ourselves at such close quarters."

As he sat back down on the bedding beside her, Caitlin poked him with her elbow and insisted, "Garn, the two of yez were riding together for days and nights. You'll niver convince me she niver noticed thim broad shoulders and bedroom eyes that go with your . . . fire hose."

He let her hold the lit cheroot and helped himself with a gulp of canned beans, sipping from the can as if it was a beer schooner. Then he pointed out, "Whatever might have happened betwixt me and a lady who ain't here to defend herself, it never took place as we were riding along any trail. Get comfortable and haul a blanket up over you if you like, but let's not even talk about getting more comfortable than that. There's no sense teasing ourselves with spicy conversations when we could come upon more rapids any minute either."

She shyly suggested, "We could pull over to a sandbar

for just a few plisant minutes, if it's really uncomfortable you are.''

Longarm swallowed more beans, handed her the can, and took his smoke back as he said, ''We could. But we ain't fixing to, no offense. Like I just told you, one of the few advantages we have on Redfern and Cartier is that they're on dry land and we ain't. I've no idea where they'd be right now. But they've doubtless ridden far enough to feel safer and more uncomfortable than when they started running. They ain't worried about anybody chasing them along that coach route because they'll keep making certain they're riding the only fresh mounts on tap. They know Malone could have made it in to Durango by this time and wired the law in the Mormon Delta, the long way round. But they know nobody out here in the *middle* has any way to send or receive any telegraph messages. Meanwhile, like I said, they've been riding for hours and that do get tedious. A rider would have to be made of more heroic stuff than your average crook to stay in the saddle all the way from Turner's Gap to Glen Canyon. They ain't pony express riders. They're surely going to take more than one good trail break. That's why we can't afford to, much as you know I'd love to. Like the turtle told that rabbit, slow and steady does it. Put your head down and catch some sleep, if you've a mind to. I'll wake you up if I hear trouble round the bend.''

Caitlin laughed, a mite bitterly, and finished the can of beans. Then she reclined across the bedding on one side, her ample hip a monument to mutual frustration, and pulled a flannel blanket up over her denim smock without a word.

Some women were like that when you wouldn't take cruel advantage of their helpless condition.

They swirled on quite a while as the calm stretches grew longer at a lower level betwixt the ever more imposing canyon walls.

The seldom-mentioned Rio San Juan would have been

considered one hell of a river in its own right if it had flowed through way more settled country to some sea, rather than forming a tributary of the more famous Colorado.

The Colorado and its Grand Canyon, further downstream, tended to low-rate all the lesser but still impressive scenery further north.

Longarm had been over some of it. He knew there were natural archways bigger than that famous natural bridge in Old Virginia. The swamping pillars of a vast flat some called the Monument Valley made all the cathedrals of the old countries look like dollhouses, whilst the Glen Canyon they were headed for would have been famous as the Grand Canyon if the Grand Canyon hadn't been so much bigger. Longarm had been up the Glen Canyon a spell back, after other crooks. So he knew it made the famous Royal Gorge of the Rockies look tame. There were heaps of places a man on the run could hide out in the depths of the canyon lands. There were scattered Mormon settlements as well. But Longarm was betting on them wanting to cross the Colorado and get on over to the far more settled country a hundred miles to the west. Two nondescript but obviously Gentile strangers would stick out like sore thumbs in the smaller, tighter Mormon communites this side of, say, Sevier Junction.

The moon was over to the west now, when you could see it when the canyon walls curved left or right. As it got lower it actually shed more light between the layers of sandstone and shale by bouncing off some limestone, higher up. But Longarm knew there were limits to that effect, and it figured to get black as a bitch down here on the water before dawn.

He said so when he had to wake Caitlin up. She said she could hear the damned blather ahead and, to his relief, she was one of those rare folk who woke up all the way fairly sudden. He figured it might go with managing a relay sta-

140

tion. With coaches running one way by day and the other by night, both in a hurry to be serviced, albeit, of course, you'd have many a dull hour between to bake meat pies and wish you could get laid.

They ran the rapid stretch without incident and Caitlin suggested he take her place in the bedding while she stood watch. He was sorely tempted, but he never did. They hit another stretch of rapids and poled over to the bank to play the float down a really bad series of shallow falls on the rope, with the two of them putting their backs into it against the current.

After that rough stretch they floated on smoother but possibly faster water. Like all the other main channels through the canyons of the Colorado Plateau, the San Juan kept picking up more water, from mere springs trickling down its canyon walls to side canyons rating names of their own, such as the Butter Wash, Crumb Creek, and really big Chinle, flowing north out of Navaho Country. Thinking about that wide, well-watered Chinle Valley and some other gals he'd met riding up it didn't calm a grown man's cravings worth spit.

They knew they were well west of all the main tributaries of the San Juan by the time it got really dark down their way. The only light came from the slightly lighter shade of starry blackness between the coal-black canyon walls to either side. Starlight wasn't half as bright as it looked to eyes adjusted to darkness. You didn't see stars in the daytime, even though they were there, just as bright, because the brightness of a star was no brighter than the blueness of a clear blue sky. Despite their twinkles, stars shed as much light after sundown as a speck of daylight sky that same size and shape, which wasn't all that much, now that they really needed some.

He couldn't read his pocket watch. There wasn't a big enough slice of sky above them for him to guess the time by the rotation of the Little Dipper around the fixed point of the North Star. But by guess and what was either the Dog Star or a planet off to their west he decided it was going on four in the morning when they heard the roar of falling water ahead and poled over to hit sheer stone walls and then a fortunate stretch of sandy beach tucked into a bend above what had to be a serious problem.

They hauled one end of the float up on the little patch of terra firma. Then Longarm struck a match and explored downstream. The sand gave way to more sheer rock, scoured by rapid muddy water. He struck a second wax match and peered up the wall to make out what might or might not have been a ledge at higher level. He returned to Caitlin by their log float to report, "It don't look good, either way. We can risk running what sounds like serious rapids in pitch-darkness, and mayhaps kill our fool selves, or we can wait here for more light on the subject and risk them killers getting away!"

She sank down to her knees on the tarp she'd spread across the sand, closer to the canyon wall, and said, "You go over a waterfall in the dark all you want to. I'm for staying here until I can see what I'd be after doing! It can't be all that long before dawn, and for all we know we may have to climb out of this sewer instead of following it any further!"

He sighed and said, "When you're right, you're right. Might your stage line have anybody posted near that ford across the Colorado in the Glen Canyon?"

As he sank down beside her on the tarp and reached for another smoke she told him, "Nobody *fords* the *Colorado*. It's a ferry raft an auld Mormon runs back and forth near the junction of the Glen Canyon and the Escalante. As I've warned you more than once, that's at least ten miles above the place we'll be after joining the Colorado and all and all."

He thumbnailed a match aflame to light the cheroot. He never lit it when he saw the way her big blue eyes were smiling at him in the flickering match light. He shook it out and got rid of his hat and cheroot as he reached out to her. She swayed his way to meet him, and then they were flat on the tarp and Caitlin was sobbing, "Yes! Yes! Yes!" as he ran his free hand up under her loose denim smock to find nothing in the way as he slid his palm up the inside of a big smooth thigh 'til his thumb parted what had to be a flaming red thatch around her fully aroused moist clit.

She moaned, "Take off your clothes, or at least that auld gun, before you shove it to me, *mo cushla*!"

So he did and it was worth the wait as he rolled atop her, buck naked, to discover she'd pulled her smock off over her red curls to welcome him in just her boots, with her big thighs opened wide and, thanks to the size of her firm rump, no need for a pillow under her to take him deep at an ideal angle.

Her vagina was tight for such a strapping mature woman, and warm and wet next to her smooth cool skin. Then it was all he could do to stay aboard and keep it in her as old Caitlin seemed to go loco under him, doing not only all the work, but bumping and grinding more than required to move the full length of his old organ grinder in and out of her, hard and fast. She moaned, "Oh, yes, me too!" when she felt him ejaculating in her. It didn't matter whether a man went limp in her strong arms or not as the powerful Caitlin kept bouncing him in her wide-open lap.

After she'd climaxed, herself, and insisted on getting on top to rest with it up inside her, she spoiled it some by resting her big tits on his bare chest and purring, "Could that English girl keep it hard for you this long and all and all?"

Longarm didn't exactly feel himself going soft. Few men would have in that position. But he did feel a mite pissed as he answered, "Damn it, honey, it ain't polite to gossip about old friends at times you've got your dong soaking in another. I never told you I'd even held hands with Miss

Phaedra and I doubt she mentioned my duration to you either! So what makes you so sure about Miss Phaedra and me?''

Caitlin laughed dirty, contracted, and confided, ''You told me the two of you caught Tom Cartier by surprise on a wagon trace through the chaparral west of my station. And what might the two of yez have been up to, down in the bushes, as a rider on the lookout rode your way?''

He could almost make out her grinning face as he scowled up at her. He said, ''Never mind what other gals were doing in private on their own time. It's starting to get lighter. It must be getting on to daybreak. We'd best get dressed and see about getting past that rough water ahead.''

She sighed and said, ''I can see you better too, and sure I was right about thim shoulders. It moit be safer to wait 'til it's a bit lighter, and can't we just take time for one more jig-a-jig-jig?''

He decided they could, as long as they made it mighty fast. So she rolled off him to lower her carrottopped head to the tarp and present her big rump to the stars, or anyone else who wanted to gaze down on it.

So Longarm agreed that was about as quick a way as there was and mounted her from behind to pound her good and suddenly laugh like hell.

She pouted, ''Is it me big ass you'd be after laughing at?''

He chuckled and replied, ''It just hit me that I'd never fully understood them words of 'One Ball Riley' before.''

Caitlin laughed too as he pounded away, loudly singing,

> ''Jig-a-jig here, jig-a-jig there.
> Jig-a-jig-jig for the Riley's daughter.
> Jig-a-jig-jig, balls and all!
> Rub-a-dub-dub, shag on!''

Chapter 17

It was still early morning but bright daylight when their float suddenly swirled around a sharp bend and began to rotate in an eddy where the San Juan met the Colorado at an acute angle. They poled for the north bank of the San Juan after Longarm pointed out his damned good reason for not wanting to try for the far side of the Colorado.

As they grounded the float he helped her ashore, saying, "That's better. We're way the hell upstream from where we'd have wound up your way, and upstream is the way we have to go. That old-timer running the ferry across, ten miles up, will see us as well no matter which bank we follow up to his crossing,"

She said she'd already said she understood all that and offered to pack their bedding and the saddlebags if he'd pack the rifle and saddle. So they started legging it north through the cathedral calm of the Glen Canyon. They hadn't gone far when they saw smoke rising above some riverside willows ahead. He'd noticed the last time he passed through these parts how settlers spilling over from the more settled and likely stricter Mormon Delta tended to settle in remote parts where irrigation water was handy to at least forty acres of fair soil.

As they forged through the willows to see more open bottomland ahead Longarm told Caitlin, "I've been thinking, and it might be best if I was to leave you for a spell with such friendly nesters as we can find."

She protested, "Aroo, it's me own mules and me own boyos they were after shooting, and it's their blood I'll be having with this grand invention of the O'Flynn!"

He told her to stick that big dragoon back in her waistband and explained, "I'd rather take 'em alive, and in any case it ain't your bravery that's at issue, honey. Like I said, I got to get on up to that crossing ahead of them and, no offense, I can walk faster on my own."

She demanded, "How would you know if you've never marched across the land with meself? Did I seem short-winded when it was jig-a-jig for the two of us last night?"

He saw the argument might be academic as they got closer to the sprawl of sod-roofed log buildings ahead. It seemed a good-sized if cozy settlement was nestled in a cove of the sculptured sandstone wall of the big canyon. From afar they looked like toy houses against the titanic cliffs rising behind them. As the two wayfarers strode closer the cliffs looked the same, while the housing and surrounding corrals, shade trees, and such seemed to grow bigger.

A dog was barking and men, women, and children came out to gawk at them as they approached. Longarm got out his badge and pinned it on to save tedious explanation. He was glad he had when a stuffy old cuss wearing a sort of pilgrim hat, full beard, and bib overalls brandished a pitchfork at them and warned them they didn't allow no drinking or gambling around there.

Longarm answered soothingly, "We ain't drunks or gamblers, mister. This lady with me works for the stage line just to your north, and I'm after the same outlaws,

146

Gentile outlaws, who've sinned considerable in the past few days. I'm Deputy U.S. Marshal Custis Long, and I'm out to arrest Lem Redfern and Tom Cartier for murder, robbery, and theft of livestock.''

The old Mormon asked, ''How can we help? Nobody should be allowed to get away with stealing livestock!''

So the helpful Mormons soon had them on their way north aboard a matched pair of Cordovan ponies, with Caitlin riding bareback, sideways, until they were out of sight around a bend and she could spread her long shapely legs to ride right with her bare crotch across her mount's spine and the hem of her blue smock halfway up her thighs.

Longarm got her to sit sidesaddle when they came to more canyon homesteads below that river crossing. They'd made good time, taking about three hours from that mouth of the San Juan to where the coach route crossed the Colorado.

The old geezers who ran an oversized raft across the brown river along a cable secured to both banks didn't know what Longarm was talking about when he asked if they'd taken Redfern and Cartier over to the west bank that morning.

They said traffic had been slow and they'd been wondering why.

Longarm asked Caitlin to explain about telegraph messages and such while he rode up the coach route to the east a ways.

When she said she wanted to come with him, Longarm said, ''I surely wish you wouldn't. I'd like to avoid gunplay down here where windows might wind up busted. Seeing it seems I have time to lay for them on the wagon trace, that's what I aim to do, and I work better alone. I know you got your own gun, and I'm sure you know how to use it, honey. But I don't want to have to worry about anyone but myself in a wild and woolly situation. So stay here and that way I'll know that anybody I feel like shooting at will likely deserve it!''

Then he'd ridden out of the tree-shaded little settlement before she could argue. The wagon trace followed the natural lay of the land as much as possible and, down here in the Glen Canyon, the lay of the land twisted considerable. The twin ruts ran upstream from the ferry settlement in a series of hairpin turns as it sought higher ground.

Longarm dismounted and led his borrowed Cordovan afoot as the route swung around a narrow treacherous-looking turn at what was now fairly high above the churning brown river's tree-shaded banks. He knew Redfern and Cartier could be most anywhere along the dusty ruts ahead, if they were coming at all. So when he came to where they'd blasted through a spur of sandstone to carve a straighter route up the east wall of the canyon he paused to study geography some.

A side canyon, running into the main one to form what they called a hanging valley, accounted for the spur of more resistant rock they'd blasted out of the way. The formation made more sense when you pictured it without the intervention of man and 40% Hercules. As things now stood, the brush-filled side canyon formed a niche about ten feet up the rough blank wall of the road cut. A handhold here and a foothold there helped Longarm get up to it with his Winchester, once he'd tethered the Cordovan to some cliff holly further down.

From his new vantage point he could see for miles and miles, some few of them important. Working some scrub juniper between himself and the bare rock face he'd just scaled, Longarm had a view up the wagon trace for a couple of curvaceous furlongs or a quarter mile. He doubted anyone riding his way down that steep and scary wagon trace could hope to spot him before he had them in his sights, point-blank, with no cover of their own.

He resisted the temptation to light a smoke as he stared

up the stage route at nothing much for a million years or so. He knew there was nothing saying they'd ever come along at all. Meanwhile Caitlin would be getting worried and that borrowed pony would be getting dry and thirsty. The sun hadn't risen above the canyon rims to the east as yet, but sooner or later it would, and the few hours of direct sunlight you got in the bottoms of these canyons more than made up for all the shade. Settlers could grow cabbages down here in the bottomlands when it was snowing atop the plateau.

He decided he'd give his notion another hour before he gave it up.

It took less than an hour to prove the point of that military genius who'd said you won a war by lasting just as long as your enemy, then hanging on for just five minutes longer. For the time was running out when two familiar riders rounded the distant bend up yonder.

"Decisions. Decisions," Longarm muttered, cocking the already primed Winchester as the two shabby riders walked their dusty mules his way.

Longarm smiled thinly and decided, "Like we figured, they didn't risk raiding that big Clay Hills home station. They went around and that's how come we beat 'em here. Them poor mules have been ridden far and long."

Lem Redfern took the lead as the ledge narrowed a mite. As a Jehu, he'd doubtless driven this route many a time and knew all the bad curves and soft shoulders. The two of them swung out of Longarm's sight as they got closer. The paradox was caused by the way their route curved inward, putting a convex bend betwixt them and Longarm's chosen ambush. Then he heard soft singing and Lem Redfern came round the bend on his jaded mule, both their heads hanging as Lem sang about tying his pecker to a tree.

So where was Cartier, the shotgun messenger murdered by the late Seth Cooper, postmortem?

Lem Redfern rode closer, then closer, until he was smack

between Longarm and the other wall of the road cut. Longarm might have let Lem pass by a ways, waiting on Cartier. But the erstwhile Jehu who'd gotten to know this route he'd driven, over and over, suddenly looked straight up at Longarm and, doubtless spotting something he wasn't used to seeing there, swung his own saddle gun up as he shouted a strangled warning!

They both fired at the same time. Lem's shot showered Longarm's hat brim with juniper juice and shattered twigs. Longarm's round hit lower and had Lem reeling in the saddle before a second shot blew him out of it, just beyond that higher spur, so he could fly ass over teakettle down the steep drop to crash down through the treetops below.

So where in thunder was his sidekick, Cartier?

Longarm called out, "It ain't too late to talk turkey, Tom. You can say Lem and the Shaw kid did all the killings, and if you return the money they just might choose to buy such horseshit!"

There came no answer.

Longarm sighed and said, "My mother told me there'd be days like this. But she never told me there'd be so many!"

Then he'd reloaded and slid back down to the wagon trace, landing in a gunfighter's crouch with his Winchester's muzzle trained up the slope.

Nothing happened. So he started easing forward, hugging the high side of the curve and trying not to crunch the dry weeds and gravel at the base of the cut.

It took more guts than he had until he reminded himself the other cuss was in the same fix, and that they, not he, had been doing all the running.

Longarm eased ever further along the convex bulge of jagged sandstone, tensely scanning each extra inch of the vertical slit of increasing view. Then he muttered, "Shit!" as he saw why Tom Cartier hadn't even seen fit to cuss back at him.

A narrow cleft, much like the one he and Phaedra had entered long ago and far away, ran all the way up from a fill the road graders had used to cross it to the cloudless morning blue above!

Longarm thought about heading back to the ferry settlement for help. But what could a handful of Mormon countryfolk do, if there was a thing anyone could do, right now, but what had to be done, God damn it!

He saw no sign of the other man's mount. He doubted anyone would drag a mule into the pumpkin after him unless he had some use for the critter in mind. So Longarm ran back down the wagon trace, untethered his borrowed pony, and led it back up the slope afoot, quietly saying, "It looks like we have to go into the pumpkin, pard. I'll tell you why as soon as I figure it out for us."

The placid saddle bronc gave him no trouble until he tried to lead it through a stone wall, from its own limited view of its canyon universe. Longarm had to tug the reins hard and risk blood on the bit with some punishing jerks before the critter came after him into the cooler dimly lit cleft betwixt water-sculpted walls no more than two yards apart in places. The floor of polished pebbles rose steeply as they wound through the almost voluptuous slit, slow, as Longarm kept pausing and listening, to hear nothing but water dripping somewhere, as if some gigantic drunk was pissing down the stairs of some vast cellar.

Then the light ahead grew brighter and Longarm was surprised to see the cleft open into a circular arena with a pretty little pond in the center and lush greenery growing on the slopes of scree all around. The weeds, brush, and trees made it look as if a small forest had come to attend a swimming meet in the center of that old Roman Colosseum.

Longarm crabbed sideways into some cover with his pony before the cuss he'd followed this far could figure out that Longarm had figured out he was boxed. For it seemed obvious they were both in the same sinkhole, a cave that had caved in after feeding that cleft behind him for longer than a mortal liked to think about. There was no other way out. Tom Cartier had likely noticed that by now. He'd likely known about this hidey-hole from his earlier travels over the stage route outside and hoped nobody else might notice it.

Tethering the pony to some aspen, Longarm moved away a few yards and called out through the fluttering leaves all around, "Hey, Tom? Like I was saying out on the road just now, you might be able to save your neck returning all that paper money and helping us tidy up a few details."

No answer.

Longarm yelled, "Come on, I know you're in here and they do say confession is good for the soul!"

A fusillade of shots rang out across the way, the reports echoing wildly off the cliffs all around. But Longarm could see by the smoke drifting through the leaves across the way where the shots had come from. He had his own rifle up to reply in kind while the sounds of Cartier's shots were still bouncing back and forth. But Longarm held his fire. A million years crept by, then a voice he'd heard on the trail with poor nearsighted Phaedra called out, "Hey, Longarm?"

Longarm didn't answer. It was a game any number could play. Cartier called plaintively, "Come on, I know I didn't get you."

Longarm didn't answer that time either. Betwixt the smoke, the yells, and the tail of Cartier's mules swishing flies like so across the way, he had the rascal's position figured closer now.

There were two ways Longarm could cut the cards, as he figured the odds. Neither was certain. Sitting tight and waiting the bastard out was likely to take all day and end in a night fight anyone might win.

The other way would be to move in, slow. The cornered

killer would be most anxious about the one way in or out. So Longarm proceeded to circle in on him from the other side, all the way around the colosseum through the tanglewood audience.

He didn't see how Cartier could get the drop on him, even if he crunched dry twigs, which was easy to avoid. The strip of cover was dense but narrow. By staying high as possible against the rock, he could see down through the branches and twigs pretty good. He kept going and going, breathing slow with his heart galloping until, sure enough, he spied the hat Tom Cartier had been wearing when he'd introduced himself as Mike Dumont.

Wanting to take him alive, Longarm threw down on the battered felt hat and yelled, ''Freeze!'' just as he saw, to his sick dismay, that the hat was stuck, empty, on some sticker brush.

The shot that rang out in reply to his demand was expected, but not from the direction it came. Longarm threw himself flat and then rolled down the slope as he tried to figure out how the son of a bitch had gotten *behind* him. The shot still echoed and he heard someone else rolling through the brush, willy-nilly, *ahead* of him! When he peered that way he saw Tom Cartier flop limply out on the gravel betwixt the slope and that little lake.

A familiar voice called out behind him, ''Did I get him with the grand invention of Himself, the O'Flynn?''

To which Longarm could only call back, ''You sure did, Caitlin. You just blew half his face off with that cannon!''

Chapter 18

Caitlin was not the only one who'd noticed Redfern's riderless mule running down the wagon trace, or heard all that gunplay. So a trio of farmers and a Mormon elder were popping out of the cleft on the far side of the sinkhole by the time Longarm had broken cover to join Caitlin and her smoking .54 dragoon near the sprawled half-headless cadaver of the late Tom Cartier.

Longarm was glad he was still wearing his badge on his lapel as the oldest Mormon introduced himself as Elder Warring and declared himself the local law.

Longarm got along with Mormons better than some because he went along with any notions that didn't seem downright unconstitutional.

The big Irish widow woman was staring down at the man she'd just killed with an ashen face but no expression as he told the three new arrivals who they were and added, "We've been chasing this one and a pal outside as road agents and worse."

Elder Warring said, "You have indeed. There's another dead Gentile on the canyon floor, outside. Was that poor soul at your feet the last of them?"

Longarm wrinkled his nose and declared, "I surely hope so. I have to go through their saddlebags before I can say for certain. Their unjust rewards for two fake robberies was two strongboxes filled with paper money."

One of the younger Mormons said, "There was no paper money in the saddlebags of that mule who just ran into our village. We naturally looked. We were trying to figure out where it had come from and who it might have belonged to when we heard all the shooting up this way."

Longarm led the way across what was likely a local lovers' trysting place to where the mule Cartier had been riding stood tethered in the greenery. He untied it and led it out into the open before he looked in the saddlebags and unrolled Cartier's bedding, to find nothing but a few cans of trail grub.

He started to reach absently for a smoke, remembered in time how the Mormons, or Latter-Day Saints, felt about tobacco, and announced, "Nada. They cached the loot to lighten their loads as they tried to blue-streak for parts unknown!"

Caitlin, coming unstuck from what had been a shock to her, looked up to gasp, "Aroo and they must have buried it, anywhere along a hundred miles or more of semidesert, and how is anyone to ever find it now?"

Longarm said, "Reckon they'll have to look for it. There'd have been no point in caching the money more than halfway here. You don't *bury* paper money unless you mean to come right back for it, and I somehow suspect it might rain out this way before it would be safe for those old boys to come back and dig it up."

He turned to regard Cartier's mangled remains with distaste and added, "That one could lie when the truth was in his favor. He'd have never gone for anything as simple as buried treasure troves. They'll have planned ahead better than that."

Caitlin brightened and said, "Didn't you tell me last

night how it was Harry Bekins and his savage squaw who wuz after hatching their master plan and all and all?"

When Longarm nodded thoughtfully, Caitlin smiled for the first time since she'd killed a man and said, "That's who'd know where the money went, then! Sure, wouldn't the divvel who'd worked out the way to steal it without being suspected have a plan to get it out of this country without getting caught?"

Longarm smiled thinly and said, "Bekins *did* get caught, when his master plan fell apart. Old Ruby wasn't in on the plot too deeply, and we made that deal with her I told you about earlier. I asked her what she knew about the money. She'd heard old Lem Redfern had been told to just toss the strongbox over the side, both times, and drive on to report a daring robbery. Tom Cartier and that Sterling Shaw kid would have plenty of time to carry it off, Tom Cartier being officially killed and left behind during the first fake robbery. But that was all Ruby could tell me. She didn't know where Cartier and Shaw were supposed to take the money. She didn't think they'd left it for safekeeping at the La Plata Station, though. The whole plan was for everybody working for the stage line they'd robbed to have ironclad excuses. It would be a total waste of a mighty complexicated plot if the company dicks found even a whiff of the loot on one of the plotters. Hiding it on or about his quarters would have been too big a boo for Harry Bekins. The two I just caught up with must have been afraid to have it on them whilst riding hard as Gentile strangers through many a settlement of you Latter-Day Saints, no offense."

Elder Warring allowed he wasn't offended and asked where Longarm figured all that money might be, in that case.

Longarm said, "I can't say, yet, whether they planned to come all the way back for it in far off safer times or planned to have another sneak pack it out to some far off safer *place*. I'm still working on both notions."

The boss Mormon asked if there was anything more they could do to help. Mormons, Mexicans, and such could talk that way if you talked to them nice.

Longarm said, "The two mules belong to the stage line. I suspect they'll make it worth your while if you'd care for them until they can be reclaimed. I don't want to pack two dead crooks all the way to Durango just to see them buried there. Might somebody here plant them in exchange for their boots, guns, and such?"

Elder Warring said he'd see to both chores, personal. So Longarm turned wearily to Caitlin and said, "Now we'd best get both you and me back to Durango, seeing your place was burned out."

She sighed and answered, "Ain't that the truth of it all and all. But the company will be expecting us to clean up and get ready for business again, now that this crime spree would be over."

Longarm nodded but said, "Nobody's likely to make a move until we can assure 'em it's over. There's no telegraph to assure anybody until you get to one end of the long run or the other. Our best bet now would be that Clay Hills home station, just a few miles off to the east."

He turned back to Elder Warring and asked if they could fix them up with some fresh riding stock. The friendly Mormons could do better than that, once they'd led Longarm and Caitlin down by the ferry for some grub, an infomal coroner's hearing, and handshakes all around.

They provided Longarm and the big redhead with spunky ponies and an armed escort, seeing the Clay Hills were less than half a day's ride and some members of the gang could be still at large, almost anywhere, with all that money.

During a trail break at the top of the climb out of the canyon, Caitlin whispered what she'd be doing to Longarm that very moment if they hadn't had so much company. He told her not to tease dumb animals.

With a quartet of unsuspecting Mormons guarding their

virtue as well as their backs, they made it to the central home station of her stage line by noon.

They found the place forted up as for a siege. They might or might not have let Longarm in with his badge. The manager there recognized Caitlin O'Flynn as a fellow station manager, however. So in the end they even invited the Mormons in for some grub and stock water.

The bitty gray possom-face in charge of the home station hadn't forted up because he'd known what was going on. He'd learned during Indian rising that when coaches didn't seem to be coming in from either end it was time to close the shutters and break out the rifles and fire buckets.

Seated outside where it was cooler, for a change, they sat along both sides of yet another plank table and jawed over a fair dinner, the Mormons politely refusing any tea or coffee with their otherwise acceptable noon grub.

Once he'd been brought up-to-date, Possom-face agreed with Caitlin that the company, once informed by wire it was safe, would commence at both ends to restock their many outlying relay stations with fresh mules and, if need be, new roofs and hired hands.

Thanks to the quick thinking of Longarm and the help of Caitlin O'Flynn, at least half the relay stations, those to the west of the Glen Canyon crossing, had been spared the savagery of the two hard-riding killers. But when Caitlin pointed out how that meant they could make Sevier Junction at the west end of the line way faster than if they pushed on for Durango with no fresh stock to change to, Longarm shook his head and told her, "I thought about that before you did, no offense. The action left figures to be way closer to Durango. I don't aim to save mayhaps an extra day in the saddle to wind up stuck at the wrong end of your stage line after I wire everybody and then my boss naturally wires me to get back to Durango and finish the chore he sent me to manage in the first place!"

Longarm turned to the old possom-face to ask about

some fresh mules, allowing the Mormon hands to head home with their own Mormon ponies.

The home station manager had mules to spare and then some, thanks to no coaches passing through, either way. But he showed he was more than a mule wrangler when he pointed out, "It's going to take the two of you at least three times as long without fresh stock to change to every ninety minutes or so."

Caitlin nodded and said, not looking at Longarm as her cheeks glowed just a mite, "I make it three days in the saddle and two nights on the ground along the way and all and all."

Her fellow travel expert replied, "That's about the size of it, and we don't know what's out there betwixt here and Durango, thanks to the murderous pair who rode it west last night! I'd like to send some of my boys and a buckboard loaded with grub, bandages, and such along with you, Deputy Long. They shouldn't slow you down and may well come in handy if you come across either survivors in need of help or more of them road agents."

Caitlin kicked him under the table. Longarm still allowed he'd go along with such a sensible suggestion. So they finished up with extra black coffee for everyone but the Mormons and got cracking.

As they were fixing Caitlin up with a proper lady's saddle from their tack room, the big Irish gal managed to get Longarm off to one side long enough to whisper, "Have you lost interest in me big titties so soon, you brute? Sure, how are we to be after jig-a-jigging along the way, now that you've invited all these others to be coming along with us?"

Longarm whispered back, "Very discreet, after dark. You just said we'd likely spend two nights on the trail, and how was I to refuse when the notion makes good sense? We're as likely to wish we'd left here with more than one buckboard if those killers shot more than one wagon load for us to carry on to Durango!''

So Caitlin dropped the matter for the moment, and they were on their way east within the hour, pacing their frisky mules to carry them and haul that buckboard as if Longarm had been leading an eight man and one woman cavalry patrol. For a horse or mule that had to carry or haul all day would surely flounder the second day if you tried to get more than thirty-odd miles out of it in warm weather.

A fast horse or mule can run twice as fast as a top human athlete. But it trots at about the same speed and walks a tad *slower* than an athletic rider might. It can only run a mile or so without stopping and, like a human marathon runner, it's through for the day and some days to follow after *pushing* just under thirty miles. So as many a disgruntled infantryman had observed on many occasions, the only good reason for officers and the cavalry to ride was that they got there about the same time with more spring left in their legs and mayhaps a slightly heavier load than they could have packed that far on their own backs.

Starting as late in the day as they had, they'd only made it to the next relay station east before sundown. The station manager, his wife and crew were alive and well, but stranded on foot. Cartier and Redfern had hit in the wee small hours, taking fresh stock and shooting the rest in a ferocious fusillade before anyone inside had managed to get out of bed.

Longarm smiled sheepishly at Caitlin when everyone but the two of them seemed to think the Durango-bound relief column ought to bed down safely indoors under a solid roof.

After Caitlin and the station keeper's wife had washed and dried the supper dishes, the big redhead caught Longarm's eye and he somehow knew he ought to excuse himself from the gathering around the stove in the front room to follow her out into the moonlight.

160

One of the station hands had been posted nearby with a Spencer repeater. So Longarm told the kid that he and the lady were going for a stroll to settle their stomachs.

They were soon buck naked on top of her denim smock, down in some waist-high chaparral. As she thrust her heroic hips upward in time with his downstrokes, Caitlin laughed like a mean little kid and confessed it made her feel dirty as Queen Mab's muc, who'd apparently been a pig belonging to a fairy queen in pagan times, and he had to warn her to keep it down unless she was willing to *really* enjoy some dog-style humping.

He warned, "It would be cruel and unusual punishment of the innocent if we asked them other healthy young gents not to ask for sloppy seconds, all the way to Durango, once they knew you liked to rut like a sow!"

She told him not to call her names and just get on with it. So he did, and then they did it again, twice more, before they went back inside, with Caitlin looking so innocent Longarm had a tough time with his own poker face.

They didn't dare try that again when they had to camp a second night along the trail, with a big campfire blazing and Longarm having to go along with the suggestion of night pickets. Any member of the party could naturally go off into the chaparral *alone* for a few minutes at a time, everyone there understanding the laws of nature. But they'd have had a time convincing anyone they were walking off hand and hand to take a leak together, prim and proper.

So the best Caitlin could manage was a whispered threat to kiss him all over his bare hide when she got him to that hotel in Durango.

Longarm doubted she'd want to hear he'd told the petite Phaedra Thorne to wait for him at that same hotel. You could only eat an apple a bite at a time and cross your bridges when you got to them.

So Longarm held his tongue and bided his time and, sure enough, as all things good and bad must end, their long weary ride finally ended in Durango with the dead and wounded they'd picked up along the way.

Their bedraggled arrival on the outskirts of town naturally drew the attention of a considerable crowd, including Deputy Malone and the boss he worked for, Sheriff Harper of La Plata County.

As Malone introduced everyone, Longarm told Malone, "No offense, but I'd like to wrap this up and get back to my own chores. We had to kill two of the gang over in the Utah Territory and I'll do the paperwork on them. But tell me something, Kevin. Ain't the scene of them two fake robberies and one killing, Turner's Gap, inside your jurisdiction?"

Sheriff Harper allowed, sort of pompously, that it surely was.

Longarm said, "That's what I was counting on. Seeing it was plotted and mostly carried out in your jurisdiction, with an election coming up, I'd be obliged and you'd be doing us both a favor, Sheriff, if you'd arrest the Widow O'Flynn, here, on the charge of aiding and abetting. I got personal reasons for not wanting to arrest her, federal. So I'm letting her have Attempted Murder on the house."

Chapter 19

Nobody wanted to pistol-whip a woman. So it took four men, and they all suffered bruises by the time they had the screaming and spitting Caitlin O'Flynn in handcuffs and on her way over to the county jail.

Once they had her safely in a patent cell, shaking the bars like a caged she-bear and wailing about murder and rape, Sheriff Harper led the way to a quieter room out front and found a bottle filed under W to pour nerve-settling drinks for Longarm, Malone, and the two junior deputies who'd just risked their nuts and eyeballs in upholding the law.

Handing Longarm a hotel tumbler containing more rye whisky than a sensible drinker might have poured for himself, Sheriff Harper said, "I sure wish you'd tell me why we just put ourselves through all that cussing and fussing just now. You say the raving she-male lunatic was out to kill you, old son?"

Longarm took a swig, feeling the need of it, before he modestly replied, "I reckon she felt mixed emotions about me. Her aiming at me and hitting Tom Cartier instead comes late in the story. It might make more sense if I started at the beginning.''

Kevin Malone said, ''I've already told everyone what you said about a famous road agent dying in private at Harry Bekins's relay station. Indian Ruby backs you up about fat Harry conspiring with Redfern and Cartier. She put her X to a written statement, over to the Bureau of Indian Affairs, before they sent her packing to the South Ute Reserve.''

Malone swallowed some rye to improve his voice and added, ''Ruby agrees they recruited that ornery kid, Sterling Shaw, when he got out of prison and hit up Harry for a job. The stage line wouldn't have approved of that, of course. But they figured they could use an extra gun waddie. Ruby says their four station hands were partly in on it, for more modest shares.''

Sheriff Harper said, ''We still picked the young rascals up. Got a few modest statements out of them. Bekins was too slick to tell them more than they needed to know.''

Longarm started to mention some other station hands they might as well bring in. But he didn't want to get ahead of his story.

Deputy Malone said, ''All right, we know they staged that first wild robbery and faked the killing of Tom Cartier over in Turner's Gap. How does that newspaper gal, Miss Thorne, fit in?''

''Innocent,'' Longarm replied. ''Her being a quick sketcher for that London newspaper was just icing on their cake, or shithouse luck, to mix my poetic explanations. Had she never been aboard that coach with her sketch pad, them other survivors would have reported the same bare-ass kachina dancer as the killer of poor Tom Cartier. It was really young Sterling Shaw with that mask, them ink lines, and a hard-on. I wasn't there. So I can't say whether he really had to kill that Mormon passenger or not. I know for a fact he never killed Cartier. The two of them lit out with the

164

money after old Redfern drove on to report he'd been robbed.''

"I see it all now!" volunteered a younger deputy who didn't see at all. He still said, "They lit out for the Mesa Verde with the loot to hide it somewhere in them cliff dwellers' ruins, right?"

Malone said, "Wrong. I just said we had all that figured out. They knew the company dicks always suspect an inside job. So they figured they'd better have Lem Redfern die at the hands of a desperado before any lawman, public or private, got warm. They staged what seemed an *attempted* robbery near the scene of the first one, to account for the buckshot in the real Seth Cooper when we found him, and to get us all to go looking for him so's to find him. Indian Ruby and one of the station hands who doesn't cotton to a long prison sentence have already confirmed all that. The plan was for Cartier, Shaw, and Redfern himself to stage one last robbery, letting their secret pal, Dick Lloyd, drive the coach and confirming witnesses on whilst the robbers and their victim lit out with the loot, staying smack on the wagon trace to keep anyone from cutting their brazen trail!"

Sheriff Harper poured himself more nerve medicine as he shook his head and marveled, "Bold as brass! That young English lady told me how Tom Cartier bluffed his way past you on the trail that time, thanks to her poor eyesight and you having never met him when he was supposed to be alive."

"That was a lead I failed to follow up on," Longarm confessed. He finished his snort and stood still for a second helping while he told them, "Cartier gave a false name and said Caitlin O'Flynn would back his play. He meant it. She would have. But I failed to take him up on the offer, and by the time we rode all over Robin Hood's Barn and I *had* the chance to ask about the mysterious stranger at the Rio

165

Manco relay station, they'd had plenty of time to get together and change answers.''

Malone shook his head like a bull with a fly betwixt its horns and said, ''I'll take your word she was in on it with Bekins and the rest of the bunch. But it sure gets complex-icated as you deal in all them extra players. Don't it reduce their winnings if they all have to share the pot in the end?''

Longarm nodded soberly and said, ''Bekins never took Caitlin O'Flynn into his confidences. She was running an-other station a ninety-minute ride away and they barely knew one another. That was the beauty of a *second* plot by Cartier and Redfern. Passing through every other day to change teams and admire her meat pies, amongst other charms, they knew no company dicks were likely to suspect her of *holding the money* for them.''

Malone gasped, ''Jesus H. Christ! You mean they were planning to just double-cross Harry Bekins and keep it all?''

Longarm nodded and said, ''Ruby told me they'd been fussing about the fat man's notion he rated the lion's share. Their newer plot was less involved and even safer. They went along with Harry's instructions to a point. Cartier and the Shaw kid decoyed us over to the Mesa Verde. We can't ask none of 'em now. But I figure the two of them split up at the Rio Manco like we suspected. Young Shaw was sup-posed to lead us a merry chase in that Mex outfit, which was described but never used in any robbery. We'll never know for certain whether the double-crossers meant to sac-rifice Sterling Shaw or not. It wouldn't have mattered to them, had we taken him alive, whether he knew enough to put Bekins and Lloyd in jail or not. I'm sure they never told the kid about their other plans.''

''Which were?'' Sheriff Harper asked.

''To get away clean with all the money, of course,'' said Longarm. He placed his palm over his tumbler to refuse a third snort while he said, ''Like I said, Cartier and Redfern knew Caitlin O'Flynn better than Bekins, Lloyd, or any of the others in on the original plot.''

"In the biblical sense?" asked Deputy Malone, who'd enjoyed some of the redhead's tasty cooking.

Longarm shrugged and said, "I doubt we'll ever know that for sure. You heard some of her wild accusations of seduction and rape just now. Suffice it to say, Cartier left Shaw to play tag with us and help us find the mummy of that tattooed New Zealander. The original plan was for someone to find it later than we did. But it didn't matter to the ones out to double-cross their mastermind. I spooked Sterling Shaw to an earlier death than planned, and by sheer luck we stumbled over the late road agent, Seth Cooper, a tad early.''

Malone said, "I've been meaning to ask you about that. Whatever possessed you and that newspaper gal to go poking about back in them gloomy tunnels so early on?"

Longarm answered soberly, "She asked what was back there. Reckon you could say she has a nose for news. However we managed, we got a mite ahead of their master plan by finishing up and heading back a day or so earlier than we were supposed to. Meanwhile, with Lem Redfern and Dick Lloyd heading west with a second heavy load of paper money, they felt they had no choice but to stage the second robbery as planned.''

Malone said, "Hold on. Caitlin O'Flynn must have known the cat was out of the bag. We passed through her relay station just ahead of the coach that afternoon!"

Longarm shook his head and said, "None of us had said anything to tell her we suspected anything. None of us *did* before we got to the next station and I recognized the late Tom Cartier from Miss Phaedra Thorne's fine sketch of her shotgun messenger, drawn before he was said to have died. Once I knew I'd been flimflammed by such a barefaced liar I began to put things together, fast. There was only one way Lem Redfern could have reported his shotgun messenger dead, if he wasn't dead. I was anxious to ask old Lem about that when his coach rolled in with Lloyd driving. You were there, Malone, when I confessed my doubts about another barefaced liar being killed by outlaws nobody else had really laid eyes on. I don't know whether they wanted us to catch Lloyd, Bekins, and the rest of the bunch at this end. I doubt they gave a fig either way, as long as none of them knew about their *second* plot with Caitlin O'Flynn and two of her station hands. You're going to want to send somebody out to pick up the two they didn't kill, by the way. I wrote down their names for you as we passed through the half burnt station. But let me hand 'em over after you have a better grasp on what they done.''

Nobody argued, so he continued, ''After they staged that second noisy robbery in Turner's Gap, with Redfern just handing the ribbons to Lloyd and dropping off with the strongbox, Redfern and Cartier backtracked along the wagon trace, mixing their sign up with total confusion, and delivered their spoils to the Widow O'Flynn. You or the company dicks ought to find it somewhere on the premises, whether you get any of her hired hands to talk or not. They're likely still scared of her. She or the fake dead men shot the two boys who couldn't be trusted with secrets. Then they shot the extra mules in the corral and set fire to the place so's she could play victim too.''

He got out some cheroots and offered around as he explained, ''If you'll think back to the wild scene at the La Plata Station, Malone, you'll remember I lit out hasty after the rascals, even though, if the truth be told, I only knew the half of it.''

He thumbnailed a match head to light Sheriff Harper's cheroot as he admitted, ''I accepted Miss Caitlin's tale of woe when I rode in on a spent mule. Knowing I'd never catch 'em on the wagon trace now, I went after 'em Tom Sawyer style—I'll give the details in my written report— and got to the Glen Canyon ahead of them with Miss Caitlin's help. She saw she had to leap aboard the same raft with my rifle and me if she was to be of any help to her true loves, Lem and Tom.''

That same young deputy leered and said, ''Hot damn, is that why she was just now accusing you of raping her out on that river?''

Longarm answered, ''Going down the rapids on a raft? She helped me run many a rapid, sincere. She had no choice. Frank or Jesse would have helped me stay right-side-up as they kept some true feelings to themselves. She tried more than once to slow me down, now that I study back on it, but I reckon she was hoping all the while that her secret pals would beat us to the Colorado, cross it, and be on their way faster than I could hope to follow by the time I cut their trail. It would have been dumb of her to back-shoot me if she didn't have to. The plan was for her to act her part as a fellow victim, sit on the money until things cooled off, and rejoin them with it, somewhere they'd never mentioned to Bekins, Ruby, or anyone else!''

Sheriff Harper said, ''Reminds me of my first wife. What gave the gal away to you, pard?''

Longarm said, ''A little of this and a dash of that, the way we all have to put such puzzles together. I wondered right off how she'd ever managed to skim a .54 slug so close to my back and hit Tom Cartier in the face with it, in thick cover. A few moments later, as we searched Cartier's possibles in vain for any sign of that money, I noticed some cans of British Army bully beef amidst his trail rations. I'd tasted the same in the past. I suddenly saw why Miss Caitlin's famous meat pies tasted different as well as delicious. Bully beef tastes a lot like corned beef. Both are cheaper than fresh meat, but folk who grow up on such seasoned beef learn to like it better than fresh.''

Sheriff Harper drew thoughtfully on the cheroot Longarm have given him and said, ''I dunno. I'd be suspicious of my first wife's aim if she'd shot a man I was facing, from behind my back. But heaps of folk eat bully beef. You just said it was cheap. Who's to say she gave it to them as they were passing through her station?''

Longarm answered simply, ''Nobody. There's more. Like I said, I got to suspecting everybody with any possible connection with the case, once my suspicions were aroused. We call what I did with them the process of eliminating. I kept suspecting and setting folk aside when they just wouldn't work. The more I considered Miss Caitlin, the more she worked. Aside from there being nothing to prove she couldn't be guilty, she made one real slip. She covered up clever as soon as I asked how she knew so much. But she had to have gossiped with Cartier to know so much about things I'd as soon not talk about.''

''You mean you and that English gal?'' asked Malone.

Longarm said, ''I just said I wasn't aiming to gossip about anything but Caitlin O'Flynn. She asked me something that told me she must have been talking to that lying Tom Cartier, after he'd met up with me and another suspect out in the chaparral.''

''You suspected Miss Thorne too?'' gasped Malone.

To which Longarm drily replied, ''I suspected you, your riders, and President Hayes until, like I said, I had to eliminate you one way or another. But Caitlin O'Flynn didn't *have* any ironclad alibi for not knowing Tom Cartier before or after he'd been officially killed by a dead New Zealander with a bad rep. Her glib excuse for knowing about some postmortem travels kept nagging at me and nagging at me *before* she had to excuse some mighty suspicious shooting!''

Malone said Longarm was sure cynical about friendly acting ladies.

Longarm shrugged and said, ''Once bitten, twice shy. Whether she was in on it or not will depend on where you find the money. I'm going to feel mighty foolish if you county lawmen never find it on or about her relay station by the Rio Manco. If it ain't there, there's no way she could be found guilty of Criminal Conspiracy. If you find it, there's no way she can beat the charge. In either case, no county court would have any use for my testimony and I got other fish to fry. How soon might I take Crusher Cosgrove back to Denver with me?''

The sheriff said they had his federal want in that same quarantined cell at their company lockup, not the county jail. So Longarm allowed he'd take it up with the D&RGW.

But as he was untethering his mount out front, a brown-haired priss in a seersucker suit-dress dashed out of the courthouse to declare her intent of hauling him back inside because they still needed him.

Longarm turned and ticked his hat brim to the lady, politely asking who still needed him, seeing he'd just jawed all he aimed to with their county sheriff.

The gal turned out to be the personal secretary of their county prosecutor. He'd sent her to fetch Longarm back for a full statement, the coming fall being election time for him as well.

Longarm took a deep breath and let it out, choosing his words with consideration for her delicate ears as he confided, ''You tell your boss for me that he don't want me anywheres near when it comes time to try the Widow O'Flynn and them others. I went to some trouble to let the county make all the arrests because I never wanted to be pestered by lawyers to begin with and, if you must know, I may have compromised myself as an arresting officer.''

She must have been to law school. She blushed but didn't look away as she demanded, ''Do you mean to imply you may have had carnal knowledge of that female suspect, Caitlin O'Flynn?''

Longarm said, ''I screwed her, more than once, if that's what your boss wants me to attest to in writing.''

The secretary blushed beet-red, allowed she doubted that very much, and ran back inside as Longarm muttered, "Ask personal questions and you'll get straight answers, you nosey little thing!"

Chapter 20

Both the county sawbones and the baby doctor Longarm had enlisted agreed Crusher Cosgrove was over the measles, but that another weekend in quarantine was the least he owed the rest of the world.

Longarm felt no call to ride a lop-eared mule around a small town. So he parted with it friendly at the stagecoach terminal and tipped one of the hostlers to cart the borrowed roping saddle back to the sheriff's stable whenever he had the time.

Longarm strode next to the Western Union, where he found a heap of messages waiting for him. Most were from his boss, Billy Vail, who wanted to know where in thunder he was and threatened to fire him if he didn't answer mighty sudden.

But the wire that had just come in read, "REPORTER CRAWFORD OF DENVER POST JUST TOLD ME STOP YOU DONE GOOD STOP NOW GET YOURSELF AND PRISONER BACK HERE YOU DELETED BY WESTERN UNION STOP VAIL"

Longarm chuckled, ripped a telegram blank off the pad atop the counter, and assured his home office he and the soon-to-be-late Crusher Cosgrove would be boarding the Monday night train, with or without medical approval.

Then, having done his duties to the law, for the moment, Longarm went back to that hotel near the rail terminal to tell Phaedra Thorne how things had turned out, leaving some spit swapping with old Caitlin out. It seemed just as well not to bother gals with such details.

But when he got to the hotel they told him that reporter gal had checked out two days back, saying something about them wanting her to go draw pictures around the spanking new Metropolitan Museum of Art in New York City.

He asked if she'd perchance left any messages for anybody. They said she hadn't. Longarm said in that case they could hire him his own room upstairs. So they did.

Longarm put the key in his pocket and went next door to the hotel dining room, muttering, "Perfidy, thy name is Woman. After all that mushy talk you just have to face the facts, old son. She was only out to sate her lust with your fair white body. She never meant to take you back to London town with her at all."

The drab waitress gal who came over to his table with a pencil stuck in her bun asked him what was so funny. He doubted she really wanted to know, so he told her he was just remembering a joke and asked if she could fix him up with a steak smothered in real Mexican chili beans.

She said, "We can try. But to tell the truth they serve really hot stuff at that chili parlor across the way. What's the joke?"

He grinned up at her to reply, "It ain't a proper joke to repeat to a lady. I recall the chili parlor you just mentioned. I et there the last time I was in town. You're right about their spicy grub, but to tell the truth I found the . . . ah, atmosphere depressing?"

The hotel waitress nodded soberly and said, "You heard about poor Selma Larsson, eh?"

Longarm chose his words carefully before he replied in

174

as casual a tone as he could manage, "Big blond gal slinging hash across the way?"

The drab on this side of the street said, "Not no more. She was murdered by her true love, just last night. Seems he found out she'd been untrue to him whilst he was away on business."

Longarm swallowed hard and said, "I reckon fried eggs over that steak would set calmer inside a man, after all. You say that aspiring cattle baron killed that other waitress? I sure hope he ain't running loose around town at the moment."

The waitress shook her drab head and said, "I can remember fried over T-bone without writing it down. They got her in the funeral parlor up by the courthouse and him in the jail behind it. How come I have to tell you all this? Weren't you in town when that lovelorn loon pumped five bullets into that loose-living blonde? I heard the shots in my room on the other side of the tracks and this hotel is closer!"

Longarm explained he'd just checked into the hotel after some days on the trail. She said she'd been wondering why he looked so much like a hobo if he could afford a hotel room and fried over T-bone. Then she sauntered back to the kitchen to fill his order, not bothering to wiggle her ass. So Longarm knew it was time he got his fool self to a good barber. For when even the homely ones started treating you like you weren't worth looking at, you weren't worth looking at.

Longarm finished his light meal, left a dime tip in spite of her attitude, and ambled on out and up the street to the nearest barbershop. He saw he'd timed it right. It was well after noon but short of quitting time, so the shop wasn't crowded. Only one other customer was waiting as the bald barber was finishing a haircut and doing his best to sell the tidied up cowhand some hair restoring tonic.

Longarm hung up his hat and coat and took a seat. The

older gent seated next to him shot a worried glance his way, hesitated, and said, "They just passed a city ordinance about wearing guns in town, stranger. You, ah, ain't supposed to wear 'em."

Longarm nodded politely and got out the badge he'd put back in his wallet west of town. That seemed to ease the uneasiness in the air considerable.

As the cowhand left and the townsman rose to take his place in the chair the barber decided, "You must have been with that posse they just sent over to the Rio Manco an hour ago."

Before Longarm could answer such a dumb question the customer who'd warned him about wearing guns in Durango without just cause let out a derisive snort and told the barber, "If the man was riding with Sheriff Harper right now he wouldn't be here for a haircut, would he?"

As the barber chuckled sheepishly the townsman with obvious time on his hands winked at Longarm from the chair and said, "They got one of them station hands of the Widow O'Flynn to turn State's evidence. He said he'd lead them to where they hid two strongboxes filled with more money than there ever was, if only they'll promise not to hang him."

The barber told Longarm, "It was awful. A whole mess of folk the stage line hired to run things right for them was running things all wrong, faking robberies and murdering anyone in the way!"

Longarm allowed he'd heard as much, glad to hear nobody seemed to be jawing about his own adventures with Caitlin O'Flynn.

Since he'd just been proven right about her holding the money for Cartier and Redfern, the county would be able to sort it all out and hand out all the hard time anyone deserved. So he could set aside his own part in a situation he'd never been sent to worry about. But how come he had a hard-on over an impossible mental picture?

There was no way in hell, even if Caitlin hadn't been in jail and Phaedra hadn't been long gone, for a man to ever get the two of them up in that hired hotel bed at the same time. But, Lord have mercy, a man could daydream as he waited for a shave and haircut on a lazy afternoon and, yep, taking turns with that big strapping redhead and that tiny athletic brunette was a daydream a cut above just being on a desert island with Miss Ellen Terry or aboard a slow boat to Brazil with one of them French ballet dancers drawn by Mr. Degas.

But by the time he was having his own shave and haircut Longarm had decided to stick with dream gals he'd never met, seeing he didn't have to worry about what they really thought of him.

As they finished up the barber made the usual remark about cheapskates who waited until they were ready to stuff a pillow before they sprang for a haircut. Then he tried to sell Longarm on combing some hair restorer, made from snake oil by Indian medicine men.

Longarm laughed and said, ''I've yet to see a snake with a healthy head of hair. But you can slop some bay rum on me if it won't cost me more than a nickel extra.''

The barber did and Longarm got out of the chair feeling so slick that it seemed a shame old Phaedra wasn't waiting at that taproom to draw his picture.

Somewhere a saloon piano burst into song as Longarm headed back to his hotel, warning himself there'd be no action in that all-male taproom either. Durango just didn't seem like the sort of town you found much action in on a workaday evening. Most of the gents just getting off work would be headed home for supper. Longarm didn't feel like jawing in a rinky-dink saloon with the transients and loners who had no supper to go home to. There were times when such conversations could make *him* feel like a lonesome tumbleweed, even though he had a better excuse than your average barfly.

He had the key to his room. Experienced travelers hung on to them to save time at the lobby desk. But that evening Longarm stopped by the desk, anyway, to ask if any messages had come in for him. The desk clerk tried not to smirk as he pointed across the lobby behind Longarm. That gal in the seersucker suit, who worked for the county prosecutor, was seated in a leather armchair under one of their paper palm trees. Longarm idly wondered why he was thinking of desert islands. He hadn't liked that officious little snip at all.

As he approached her, taking off his Stetson, the secretary gal with a briefcase in her lap looked up, sort of startled, to smile and say, "That clean shave and haircut explains a lot. I'm sorry if I upset you earlier with my crudely worded personal question. They told me you were staying here and I thought I'd drop by on my way home and bring you up-to-date on recent developments."

Longarm suggested they go next door for some coffee and cake whilst she had her say.

She rose but warned she couldn't stay long as he ushered her into the dining room. That same drab waitress shot them a startled look as Longarm sat the secretary gal at a cozy corner table.

After the waitress had come over to take their order for coffee and Napoleon pastry, sniffing thoughtfully at his bay rum, the gal across the table from him said, "Caitlin O'Flynn won't be standing trial in front of a jury, so we won't be summoning any witnesses against her. She's made a full confession and thrown herself on the mercy of the court."

The little law court gal looked sort of smug. Her brown hair had copper highlights in the dining room lamplight. She confided she was the one who'd talked the big redhead into a plea bargain.

She said, "I talked to her woman to woman. Caitlin O'Flynn's not outstandingly evil. Just human, and not too well educated. As you'd guessed, it was that really wicked Tom Cartier who led her down the primrose path. He was the one who shot those two station hands they couldn't recruit to help them hide the money there. I thought you might be interested to hear that it was him, not you, Caitlin was aiming at the other morning. She said that once she saw Lem Redfern was dead she was afraid you'd take Tom Cartier alive and uncover her shame.''

The waitress brought their coffee and sweets and slammed them down with an annoyed glance at the younger secretary gal.

Longarm waited until she'd flounced off before he told the other gal, ''I told her she could have that killing on the house, since he was a killer on the run trying to gun a federal lawman. So it hardly matters if she was aiming at him or me. Had she managed to keep us in the dark about her and old Tom she'd have had less money to share. On the other hand, she must have been fairly close to one or the other of them killers. No offense, but it's been my experience that warm-natured gals led astray into a life of crime need more warmth and attention from their fellow crooks than your average fellow crook of the he-man persuasion.''

She dimpled across the table at him and allowed he'd know more about warm-natured she-crooks than herself. That waitress seemed to drift back and forth slowly, more than she needed to with the dining room less than half full at the moment. Longarm didn't blame their waitress. The conversation at their table was getting more exciting as the gal from the prosecutor's office said, ''Caitlin O'Flynn is not the only person who's been talking about you and your way with ladies behind your back, Deputy Long.''

He said his friends called him Custis and asked what she wanted him to call her.

She said, ''Miss Stewart, for now, Deputy Long. I'm not sure I approve of your way with the ladies.''

It wouldn't have been polite, or smart, to ask why she was smiling like that if she found him so disgusting. So he just asked if some other gal had been talking about him behind his back, assuring Miss Stewart he hadn't been acting forward with any gal in Durango, which was the simple truth, when you studied on it.

She demurely replied, "I know, Selma Larsson has been murdered by another lover and Miss Phaedra Thorne left town even earlier."

Longarm whistled softly and replied, "Word sure does get around in a town this size. But I doubt that newspaper gal pressed any charges on her way back east, and as for that waitress across the way, I give you my word as a man that I know nothing at all about her and her true love. He was out of town the only time I ever went near her. I was out of town when he did whatever he done to her."

Miss Stewart washed some pastry down and assured him, "I just said you won't be called as a witness. He's made a full confession and his hearing won't require a jury in open court. You weren't the only rival his true love threw in his face when he failed to satisfy her a third time. She named half a dozen who could before he finished his fifth of bourbon and emptied his .45 into her as she was dressing to go out for more excitement."

Longarm sighed and said, "Old Selma was inclined to be hasty. I'll never be able to ask her now. But I suspect she might have done some hasty shooting on her own part when she spied me sitting by a taproom window with another lady. I don't see who else it might have been. But in any case I'd barely had time to reassure her before her way richer true love found her at last. It's a shame things didn't work out better for such a warm-natured but sort of moody gal."

Then he asked how come they were jawing about old Selma if he wasn't to be drawn into her sad story.

Miss Stewart stared thoughtfully across the table at him,

sighed, and confessed, "I was curious about you. Over by the courthouse I took you for a crude unshaven saddle tramp. Yet three attractive women, who had nothing else in common, seem to have found you irresistible!"

Longarm put down his cup to say, "Aw, mush, I never run after any ladies with a club, Miss Stewart."

She answered with a puzzled smile, "I know. Caitlin O'Flynn told me she made the first move, and enjoyed the results more than she was expecting to. I'll write the late Selma Larsson off as a wayward cow town slut if you'd like to explain why that high-toned lady from the *Illustrated London News* found it so hard to stay out of the chaparral with you!"

Longarm smiled sheepishly and said, "I reckon she liked to find it hard in the chaparral. I warned her there might be gossip. You never heard a word from anybody I was bragging to, though."

She was staring at him owl-eyed as she decided, "It must be something you sprinkle in our food! I swear I was only curious when we sat down, and now I must be going lest I make a total fool of myself, you brute!"

He said he'd walk her home if she'd be a sport and let him buy her another chocolate Napoleon. So she did and what with one thing and then another it was after midnight before Longarm was up in his hired room, going at it hot and heavy with a gal who'd confessed she was curious as any other woman about men with wicked smiles and terrible reputations.

But of course it was the waitress who'd chased him upstairs after he got back from walking Miss Stewart home when the dining room shut down for the night.

Miss Stewart didn't chase him upstairs until the *next* night, after she'd heard about him and that plain-faced but mighty shapely waitress.

Watch for

**LONGARM AND THE
WHISKEY CREEK WIDOW**

232nd novel in the exciting LONGARM series
from Jove

Coming in April!

A special offer for people who enjoy reading the best Westerns published today.

If you enjoyed this book, subscribe now and get...

TWO FREE WESTERNS

A $7.00 VALUE—NO OBLIGATION

If you would like to read more of the very best, most exciting, adventurous, action-packed Westerns being published today, you'll want to subscribe to True Value's Western Home Subscription Service.

TWO FREE BOOKS

When you subscribe, we'll send you your first month's shipment of the newest and best 6 Westerns for you to preview. With your first shipment, two of these books will be yours as our introductory gift to you absolutely *FREE* (a $7.00 value), regardless of what you decide to do.

Special Subscriber Savings

When you become a True Value subscriber you'll save money several ways. First, all regular monthly selections will be billed at the low subscriber price of just $2.75 each. That's at least a savings of $4.50 each month below the publishers price. Second, there is never any shipping, handling or other hidden charges— *Free home delivery.* What's more there is no minimum number of books you must buy, you may return any selection for full credit and you can cancel your subscription at any time. A TRUE VALUE!

Mail the coupon below

To start your subscription and receive 2 FREE WESTERNS, fill out the coupon below and mail it today. We'll send your first shipment which includes 2 FREE BOOKS as soon as we receive it.
